THE RETICENT HEART

GILBERT HERNANDEZ

C • O • N • T • E • N • T • S

FANTAGRAPHICS BOOKS

FANTAGRAPHICS BOOKS
1800 Bridgegate St., Suite #101
Westlake Village, CA 91361

Editor: Gary Groth
Art Director: Dale Crain
Cover coloring: Jim Woodring
Production assistance: Doug Erb, Carol Kovinick-Hernandez,
and Mark Thompson
Typesetting: Inez M. Selleck
Production Manager: Kim Thompson

First Fantagraphics Books edition: May 1988.
10 9 8 7 6 5 4 3 2 1

ISBN: 0-930193-65-2.
Printed in the U.S.A.

The greatest era in American comic book history was the period when underground comics were in the ascendant, 1965 to 1975. During those ten years, when Crumb, Shelton, Spain, Griffith, Green, and other gifted artists came to the fore, it seemed a start was being made: that now, finally, we had a school of adult comic book creators.

But no-o-o. Nixon got out of Viet Nam, and high school and college kids didn't have to worry about going to war. They stopped protesting and revolting against the evils that remained. Within a few years the counterculture faded, to be replaced by the "Me Generation" and the yuppies, and underground comics lost their market.

The late '70s and early '80s were grim. Alternate comic book publishers still existed, but increasingly went for the same junk that Marvel and DC featured. The promise of several years ago—gone.

But as the depressing '80s run their course, things seem to be picking up. Slowly, gifted people have been emerging: the Canadian David Boswell; Drew Friedman, who sometimes illustrates the stories of his talented brother Josh; and, from Southern California, Jaime and Gilbert Hernandez.

It's a shame that the latter two are known as "the Hernandez Brothers," though they are brothers, because they usually don't collaborate. Consequently, they don't get the individual attention they deserve. Jaime's stories, set in an urban U.S. environment, deal with young people, many but by no means all of them Latino. Much of Gilbert's work takes place in Palomar, a Central American village. It's tiny, with a population of only 386, but a relatively large number of characters are featured. Most were introduced, some as children, in an earlier collection, *Heartbreak Soup and Other Stories*. Now they are young adults with families, jobs, and long-standing relationships.

The central cast of men in *Heartbreak Soup* grew up with each other. Two of them, Manuel and Toco, die in the first collection, although they are referred to here. If you aren't familiar with Palomar, "For the Love of Carmen" summarizes some of the town's history and the background of some of its leading citizens. In this story, Heraclio comes to Palomar as a teenager and falls in love with the pint-sized Carmen. He goes away to college but can't get the place or Carmen out of his mind, so he returns, gets a job teaching music, and marries her. Here and in "Holidays in the Sun," we have nice flashback sequences; during the latter the boundary between the present and the past is blurred.

"Holidays" focuses on Jesus, who had earlier freaked out, wrecked his place, inadvertently injured his kid, and then stolen a car to hide out in the mountains. His friends find him and bring him back, but he gets a prison sentence for his escapade. Here we see him incarcerated on an Alcatraz-like island, baking in the heat and having hallucinations about the beautiful women of Palomar, including Luba, the earth-mother with gigantic breasts who gives baths for a living, and gorgeous Tonantzin, always dreaming of a Hollywood career.

She gets carried away in "An American in Palomar," when photojournalist Howard Miller comes to town hoping to get a series of pictures showing the "natives" at their most charmingly naive. At first people are at least helpful. Tonantzin even gets involved sexually with him, thinking he can help her get into the movies. Eventually, though, they understand that he's got a condescending attitude toward them, and run him out of town. Ironically, he realizes later that he can't get Palomar and its people out of his system; that he's much more strongly attached to them than he knew. In "For the Love of Carmen," which comes later in the chronology, Luba and Israel argue about Miller. Heraclio, the narrator, remarks, "Even after he was long gone, I noticed a lot of folks in town were pretty mad at Miller, but I could see that most of them were just using him to vent their racist anti-white bile in public."

The subject of gringo-Latino relations has seldom been dealt with on anything but a superficial level in comics, or at least the ones I've seen. Gilbert's handling of the subject evidences his perceptiveness and tolerance. Add to these qualities those of a gifted author-illustrator and you've got a praiseworthy artist. Gilbert's writing and drawing styles have been taken from a wide variety of sources—highbrow, popular, and folk. In one panel he copies a Van Gogh painting; elsewhere Frieda Kahlo and some of Jaime's characters pop up. Some Palomarans are physically idealized, like Tonantzin and Israel; others look like Chester Gould grotesques. Seemingly disparate elements come together in his work; some of his most humorous effects come from his use of incongruity.

Throughout Gilbert displays affection for Latin American culture, urban and rural. There's an engaging unpretentiousness and warmth about the Palomar tales; you can tell the author likes his characters, whether they're straight or eccentric. A strong sense of community exists in Palomar. People look out for one another, realizing that "we're all in it together" and "one hand washes the other." Gilbert doesn't make ths point over-obviously. His people quarrel and fight plenty, but when a Palomaran is in trouble, he or she usually gets support from somewhere. Justice doesn't always carry the day in Palomar; innocent people get hurt. But when they do, I'm aware of Gilbert's concern for them. The humor and sensuality in his work have been praised, but don't overlook his compassion, his ethical sense. These are the qualities that give his work a backbone. —HARVEY PEKAR

Gilbert Hernandez

1

SUGAR 'N' SPIKES

by BETO-88

I'M VICENTE.

ONE TIME PIPO MADE ME FEEL HER HEAD. FELT LIKE ANY OL' HEAD TO ME...

THE DOCTOR DROPPED HER ON HER HEAD WHEN SHE WAS BORN BUT IT DIDN'T DO ANYTHING. DID SHE HAVE A SUPER-DUPER HARD HEAD THEN, OR A SUPER-DUPER SOFT RUBBERY HEAD, WE WONDERED? PIPO COULDN'T REMEMBER THAT FAR BACK...

EVERYBODY KNOWS THAT PIPO'S ABOUT THE BEST LOOKING GIRL IN THE WORLD, AND WE FIGURED THAT WAS BECAUSE SHE WAS DROPPED. THAT HAD TO BE IT BECAUSE HER MA AND PA ARE SO DIFFERENT LOOKING.

PIPO NEVER ACTED LIKE SHE WAS A PRETTY GIRL. YOU KNOW HOW PRETTY GIRLS USUALLY ACT. WELL, PIPO DIDN'T. ALL SHE WANTED TO DO WAS PLAY FUTBOL AND STUFF.

THOOP!

OLD GUYS, I MEAN OLD GUYS, LIKE EVEN SIXTEEN YEARS OLD OR SO, ACTED REAL NERVOUS AROUND HER, EVEN WHEN SHE WAS LITTLE. PIPO WOULD BE NICE TO THEIR FACES, BUT WHEN THEY WEREN'T LOOKING, ¿ WHEW! ?

COPYRIGHT © GILBERT HERNANDEZ -1988-

I GUESS PIPO LIKED ME A LOT WHEN WE WERE LITTLE, BECAUSE SHE WAS ALWAYS TRYING TO KISS ME AND STUFF BUT I ALWAYS RAN.

ONE TIME I LET HER KISS ME AND IT WAS ALL WARM AND GOOPY, BUT AT LEAST I DIDN'T GET SICK. ♥

The Reticent Hea

ONE TIME SOME GUY SAID **PIPO** ONLY LIKED ME BECAUSE SHE FELT SORRY FOR ME, AND BOY, DID **SHE** LET HIM HAVE IT! PIPO'S GOT PRETTY STRONG LEGS FROM PLAYING FUTBOL SO MUCH, SO SHE SOCKED AND KICKED **THE HELL** OUT OF THAT GUY TILL HE BLED FROM THE EARS! TRUE STORY, I SWEAR!

WE HAD THIS KICKING CONTEST ONCE AND I WENT FIRST. I WAS A PRETTY GOOD KICKER AND I GOT THAT SUCKER UP THERE PRETTY HIGH.

FOOPT!

JESUS WAS NEXT AND HE NEVER WAS A VERY GOOD KICKER BUT AT LEAST HE ALWAYS TRIED. HE ALWAYS HURT HIMSELF DOING STUFF, BUT HE NEVER GAVE UP AND HE NEVER GOT MAD WHEN HE COULDN'T DO SOMETHING SO GOOD. WELL, ALMOST NEVER.

OF **COURSE** JESUS' RETARDO BROTHER **TOCO** HAD TO TRY TOO, EVEN IF HE WAS TOO LITTLE AND HE'D CRY IF WE DIDN'T LET HIM, OF **COURSE**, AND OF **COURSE** HE COULDN'T DO IT EVEN IF WE GAVE HIM SIX TRIES! TCH.

ISRAEL NEVER TRIED ANYTHING HARD IN HIS WHOLE LIFE, IT SEEMED LIKE. HE MANAGED A PUSSY KICK THAT DIDN'T EVEN GO HIGHER THAN A ONE STORY HOUSE, AND WHEN WE SAID HE COULD TRY AGAIN, HE SAID NO. IT'S NOT HIS FAULT, I GUESS.

PIPO WAS NEXT SO OF COURSE SHE CLOBBERED THAT BALL UP INTO ORBIT SO HIGH THAT FOR A SECOND WE ALMOST GOT IT MIXED UP WITH THE MOON...

THOPT!

SO THEN IT WAS JUST BETWEEN ME AND HER TO SEE WHO THE KICKING CHAMP WAS. I GAVE THE NEXT ONE MY BEST...

THEN HER...

THEN ME AGAIN...

THEN HER...

THOOP FAP THOP FOOP THAP

②

FINALLY IT WAS TOO DARK TO SEE THE BALL ANY MORE, SO THE JUDGES HAD TO DECIDE ON THE WINNER. THEY PICKED WHO ELSE? *PIPO!*

CLAP CLAP

THEN, I DON'T KNOW WHY, I GOT *SUPER MAD!* I SAID THEY ONLY PICKED HER BECAUSE SHE WAS A *GIRL* AND SHE WAS *SO PRETTY* AND *EVERYBODY* LOVES PIPO AND *BLAH BLAAHH*--

I SHOULDN'T HAVE SAID THAT BECAUSE THEN SHE STARTED TO CRY. NOT LIKE WHEN YOU FALL OFF A BIKE AND YELL, BUT LIKE... I DON'T KNOW... HER CHEST WAS JUMPING LIKE WHEN YOU GET THE HICCUPS, Y'KNOW? AND HER BOTTOM LIP GOT ALL RUBBERY AND WIGGLY... AND HER EYES... I NEVER SAW EYES GET LIKE THAT IN MY WHOLE LIFE...

THE GUYS STARTED LAUGHING AND CALLING HER CRYBABY AND STUFF, SO SHE GOT MAD AND STARTED CHASING 'EM BUT SHE COULDN'T CATCH 'EM BECAUSE HER LEG WAS SO SORE FROM KICKING ALL DAY. THOSE GUYS WERE PRETTY LUCKY, YOU BET!

NEXT DAY WAS LIKE NOTHING HAPPENED THE DAY BEFORE. WE WERE ALL NICE TO EACH OTHER AND STUFF, EXCEPT ONE THING WAS DIFFERENT. ME AND PIPO COULDN'T PLAY BALL ON ACCOUNT OUR KNEES WERE TAPED UP.

PIPO STOPPED PLAYING BALL ALTOGETHER WHEN SHE STARTED WEARING A DRESS EVERYDAY. *EVERY- DAY* WEARING A DRESS! I FEEL SORRY FOR GIRLS.

I NEVER SEEN EYES GET LIKE THAT EVER BEFORE AND NEVER SINCE... I GUESS WHEN I GET OLDER I MIGHT.

I SURE HOPE I NEVER MAKE ANYBODY HAVE THOSE EYES EVER AGAIN.

CCCP

THAT'S ALL...

CCCP

The Reticent Heart

Heartbreak Soup Theater

ON ISIDRO'S BEACH

by BETO
WRITTEN LATE 85 -
FINISHED EARLY 84-

CASIMIRA'S NEVER SEEN THE OCEAN BEFORE-- WHOOP--!

YO HO HO!

HEY... DON'T GO IN TOO DEEP, GUADALUPE...!

I ALREADY LEARNED HOW TO SWIM, MOM! TIP IN TIP IN AND DORALIS ARE LEARNING; NOT ME!

YOU'RE NOT TOO SCARED FOR YOUR SWIMMING LESSON, ARE YOU, DORALIS?

NO! I WANNA SWIM! SWIM! SWIM!

≡ULP≡

C'MON TIP! TELL ME WHAT THERE IS TO BE AFRAID OF?

HOW MUCH TIME DO YOU HAVE?

Gilbert Hernandez

The Reticent Heart

Gilbert Hernandez

7

The Reticent Heart

The Reticent Heart

A MAN CAME AND MOM HAD TO TAKE OUT HER HAMMER AND HAD TO MAKE ME GIVE HIM A SANDWICH AND YOUR SODA, TIPIN TIPÍN!

OH, IT WAS ISIDRO RIVAS, TIP. HE LOOKED PRETTY BAD... I WONDER WHAT..?

ISIDRO RIVAS? OH...

IT WAS LIKE DOMINOES; FIRST HIS BUSINESS WENT BANKRUPT WHEN HE REFUSED TO SELL OUT TO A LARGER COMPANY UP NORTH...

SOON AFTER HIS WIFE RAN AWAY WITH HIS OWN BROTHER...

--ISIDRO JUST LIVES HERE ON THE BEACH NOW...HE THINKS HE OWNS IT, I'M TOLD. SHERIFF CHELO'S TRIED TO KICK HIM OFF SEVERAL TIMES, BUT-- WELL...

I-I'M COLD, MOM...

ALL RIGHT, LUPE... WE CAN EAT ON THE WAY HOME THEN...

SHOTGUN!

LET DORALIS SIT UP FRONT WITH YOU, MARICELA!

AND YOU'RE NOT SUPPOSED TO PLAY DOCTOR ON ISIDRO'S BEACH WITHOUT ASKING HIM--!

?!

!?

BETO 83 84

The Reticent Heart

COPYRIGHT © GILBERT HERNANDEZ-1984

Gilbert Hernandez

13

HERACLIO: AIR·AWK·LEO / TONANTZIN: TOE-NONT-ZEEN

The Reticent Heart

Gilbert Hernandez

VICENTE: VEE-SEN'-TEH / ISRAEL: EES'-RYE-EL / JESÚS: HEH-SOOS' / MARICELA: MARR-EE-SELL'-AH

The Reticent Heart

GUADALUPE: GWAH-DAH-LOO-PEH / DEMOÑA (DEMON GIRL): DE-MOE-NYUH / PIPO: PEE-POE / SERGIO: SAIR-HEE-O / GATO: GAH-TOE / MANUEL: MON-WELL

Gilbert Hernandez

IS PIPO STILL GABBING WITH THAT CANNONBALL SMUGGLING TRAMP?

YEAH, WHEN THEY PASSED OUT THE TITS, LUBA WAS THERE WITH A WHEELBARROW! EXPLAINS WHY THEY WERE ALL OUT WHEN LUCIA WENT FOR HER OWN --

AUGUSTÍN! LUCIA! NOW, BEHAVE!

OW!

AH, SHUT UP, PIPO! YOU'RE NOT MOM!

NO! I'M YOUR BIG SISTER! AND I HIT HARDER THAN MOM!

SO WHEN IS MY BROTHER-IN-LAW GONNA SHOW UP, PEEP?

OH, WELL, UH...YOU KNOW GATO...

CARMEN... CARMEN, I WISH YOU WOULDN'T BE SO DOWN ON LUBA. THE GIRL'S GOT ENOUGH PROBLEMS WITHOUT YOUR --

EVERYBODY'S GOT PROBLEMS, PIPO! HERS MIGHT BE RESOLVED IF SHE WOULD MARRY AND GIVE HER KIDS A FATHER.

ALL RIGHT THEN, SHORTY. WHEN ARE YOU GOING TO GIVE YOUR HERACLIO A SON?

OH, I DON'T KNOW... I GUESS WHEN YOU GIVE YOUR GATO A SON OF HIS OWN.

YOU'RE ABOUT AS FUNNY AS MUSTARD GAS, GIRL.

HOW ABOUT THESE BABOSAS TONANTZÍN WHIPPED UP, HUH?

MM. YOUR FRIEND SURE CAN COOK. SHE'S GOING TO MAKE SOMEBODY A GOOD WIFE SOMEDAY.

TONANTZÍN? MARRIED? NO, SHE LOVES HER MEN TOO MUCH... AND AS OFTEN AS POSSIBLE.

LUCIA: LOO-SEE-AH / AUGUSTÍN: OW-GOOSE-TEEN / BABOSAS (SLUGS): BAH-BOE-SAHS

Gilbert Hernandez

YI! NOW SHE'S WHAT I CALL A WOMAN!

HER? YEAH, I GUESS SHE'LL PASS FOR A MOVIE STAR...

TOLD YOU GUYS THIS TOWN HAD SOME GREAT GIRLS!

HEY, SOFIA LOREN!

HA! YOU'RE SOFIA LOREN!

SOFIA LOREN; SHIT! I SHOULD HAVE SOFIA LORENED THEM!

HEY, TIPIÑ TIPIÑ! WHO'S SOFIA LOREN?

SOFIA LOREN? WHY... WHY SIMPLY ONE OF GOD'S GREATEST GIFTS TO MANKIND...!

AN ACTRESS OF BEAUTY AND TALENT BEYOND MEASURE, SHE HOLDS A PLACE IN THE HEARTS OF ALL MEN WHO ARE FORTUNATE ENOUGH TO CROSS HER PATH...

SEÑORA LUBA SHOWED ONE OF LA LOREN'S OLD PICTURES AT THE MOVIE HOUSE JUST LAST MONTH. DIDN'T YOU SEE IT..?

NO, I NEVER HANG AROUND THAT PLACE...

SO DO YOU THINK I LOOK LIKE THIS... THIS SOFIA LOREN?

HMMM...

HEH HEH

WHAT'S SO FUNNY?

TIPIÑ TIPIÑ : TEE-PEEN' TEE-PEEN'

The Reticent Heart

HEH..I JUST NEVER NOTICED IT BEFORE...

IN HER YOUTH, OF COURSE.

WELL..! LONG AS SHE'S A GOOD ACTRESS...

...AND THEN HE SAID THAT SHE HOLDS A PLACE IN THE HEARTS OF ALL MEN WHO MAKE A PASS...OR SOMETHING LIKE THAT...

OH, TONANTZIN! TIPÍN TIPÍN SAYS THAT ABOUT ALL WOMEN! YOU KNOW THAT HE'S GOT NO TASTE!

I SWEAR, YOU BELIEVE EVERYTHING!

WELL, JUST THE SAME, I BET IF I WENT TO HOLLY-WOOD, I COULD GET WORK THERE EASY, CARMEN.

YEAH, BUT I HEAR THEY'VE GOT ENOUGH WHORES AS IT IS.

BITCH--!

WHOOP..!

THAT...CARMEN'S PROBABLY RIGHT. SOMETIMES IT DOESN'T LOOK LIKE I'LL EVER GET OUT OF THIS...THIS TOWN. I'LL STILL BE HERE SELLING FRIED BABOSAS ON THE STREET TILL I'M AN OLD HAG. SNIFF...

...UNLESS I FIND SOME RICH GUY LIKE PIPO DID...

HEY, STRANGER! HOW'D YOU LIKE TO TAKE ME AWAY FROM ALL THIS?

EVER HAVE ONE OF THOSE GOOD DAYS.?

9

Gilbert Hernandez

21

BORRO: BOAR-O / CASIMIRA: CASS-EE-MEER-AH

The Reticent Heart

Gilbert Hernandez

23

MAN, THAT FUCKING COCKSUCKER HASN'T CHANGED ONE BIT!

CAN'T IMAGINE WHY SHE EVER MARRIED THE PRICK...

SPEAKING OF WIENERS; I HAD BETTER FIND ISRAEL...

DAMN IT; DIDN'T THINK I'D GET OUT THIS LATE! HOPE LUBA'S NOT TOO MAD...

HEY..!

YOU'RE THE MORTICIAN THAT LUBA'S BEEN SEEING, EH? MORTICIAN...

HERE WE GO..!

THAT'S RIGHT, BUT FEAR NOT; I WASHED MY HANDS TWICE BEFORE COMING...

YEAH, I USED TO BE SHERIFF OF THIS TOWN, YOU KNOW? AND I'VE SEEN SOME BAD SHIT... BUT NOT LIKE YOU, EH? I'LL BET YOU'VE SEEN IT ALL, BOY!

WELL, NOT QUITE. I CAN STILL BE SURPRISED ONCE IN A WHILE.

ON THE OTHER HAND... I'LL BET YOU GET A HOLD OF SOME REAL BEAUTIES FROM TIME TO TIME ...

YEAH... JUST YOU AND A BEAUTIFUL FRESH CORPSE IN THERE ALL ALONE ...

SUCH CHARMING PEOPLE TO MEET IN PALOMAR, HUH, ARCHIE?

LUBA!?

HEY-- WAS THAT GUY FOR REAL, OR WHAT? I MEAN--

BORRO WAS TRYING TO START A FIGHT, ARCHIE; BUT HE'S NOT WORTH IT...

IF YOU SAY SO, HON...

WHAT A GORILLA...

WELL, LET'S FORGET IT. WE'RE HERE TO DANCE!

12

The Reticent Heart

OFELIA: O·FELL·EE·AH

Gilbert Hernandez

25

The Reticent Heart

Gilbert Hernandez

MARTIN EL LOCO - MAR-TEEN EL LOE-COE (THE CRAZY)

The Reticent Heart

Gilbert Hernandez

30

Gilbert Hernandez

...WELL, YOU CAN'T SEE IT IN THE DAY, BUT IT'S THERE. AND IT'S *WAY* BIGGER THAN THE EARTH!

BIGGER'N EARTH, HUH?

I WONDER HOW BIG THE PEOPLE ARE WHO LIVE THERE?

PEOPLE?! WHO SAID ANYTHING ABOUT *PEOPLE?!*

WELL, *WE* LIVE ON A PLANET, SO WHY CAN'T THEY?

¡¡¡PEOPLE???

HE'S RIGHT·· WHO *KNOWS* WHO LIVES ON THOSE PLANETS?! NOT TO MENTION THEIR *DOGS!*

HEY, SEÑORITA COSMONAUT! WHY SO DOWN?

THOSE JUDGES WERE RIGHT! I WISH THEY HAD SHUT THAT DUMB GALILEO UP FOREVER! I HATE HIM! *I HATE HIM!*

GUADALUPE! SWEETHEART, WHAT IS IT?

I'M ALL MIXED UP! EVERYTIME I THINK I GOT IT ALL FIGURED OUT SOMETHING ELSE COMES ALONG AND MIXES THINGS UP WORSE! IT'S SCARY--

GUADALUPE, LISTEN...

SOME PEOPLE DIE DEFENDING WHAT THEY BELIEVE IN, LUPE. SOME JUST GET BLOODY NOSES AND OTHERS GO TO JAIL. EVEN IF IT HURTS OUR FEELINGS OR DRIVES US CRAZY, PEOPLE HAVE TO BE ALLOWED TO SAY WHAT THEY THINK! IT'S THE ONLY WAY WE CAN BE FREE TO PURSUE THE *TRUTH!*

THAT MEANS YOU CAN *HATE* THAT OL' GALILEO ALL YOU WANT, HONEY.

DON'T CONFUSE HER, GIRL! *GALILEO* IS A FINE EXAMPLE OF COURAGE AND CONVICTIONS!

IF YOU BELIEVE THAT STORY. HE MAY HAVE BACKED DOWN IN REAL LIFE, Y'KNOW.

WHAT?

SURE. IT HAPPENED HUNDREDS OF YEARS AGO, RIGHT? WHO KNOWS HOW MUCH THE STORY'S BEEN DISTORTED SINCE THEN? YOU WANT LUPE TO BELIEVE THE *TRUTH* DON'T YOU?

HUMPHF. ALLRIGHT, SMARTY!

GUADALUPE EVENTUALLY LEARNED TO APPRECIATE THE WONDERS OF THE HEAVENS AND LATER THE GRAVITY OF GALILEO'S PLIGHT.

THEO THEN TOO ACCEPTED THE CONCEPT OF THE UNIVERSE BEING ETERNAL, IF ONLY TO SALVAGE WHAT WAS LEFT OF HIS EYESIGHT.

The END 4

The Reticent Heart

CLAVO - SPIKE

The Reticent Hear

YOW! THERE'S A WHOPPER NOW!

LOOK AT THIS GUY! HE'LL FEED ABOUT A HUNDRED PEOPLE!

HE'S NO GOOD, THEO. JUST LEAVE HIM.

NO GOOD, HAH! YOU'RE JUST JEALOUS 'CAUSE I FOUND HIM FIRST, TONANTZÍN!

THEO, THE BABOSAS WITH THE BLACK SPOTS ARE GOOD, AND THE ONES WITH GREY SPOTS ARE POISON. HE'S GREY.

I ALWAYS GET MIXED UP! I SHOULD JUST QUIT!

NOT IF YOU WANT TO TAKE SOME FRIED BABOSAS HOME TO YOUR MOM LATER, THEO.

TSK! DID THAT DIANA TAKE OFF RUNNING?

THERE SHE GOES! BOY, SHE SURE LIKES TO RUN A LOT, HUH? I WONDER HOW COME?

SHE'S LIKED TO RUN EVER SINCE SHE COULD WALK. WHO KNOWS WHY...

AT HOME DIANA VILLASEÑOR IS ONLY TONANTZÍN'S LITTLE SISTER; AT SCHOOL, SHE IS AN AVERAGE STUDENT; BUT WHEN SHE RUNS..! WHEN SHE RUNS SHE IS ZEPHYRA, ONE WITH THE WIND...

Gilbert Hernandez

WHILE DIANA BECOMES POSSESSED BY A GODDESS, TONANTZIN IS ACTUALLY NAMED AFTER GOD'S OWN MOTHER, THE PROTECTRESS OF THE EARTH, AND SHARES SOME SIMILARITIES WITH HER CELESTIAL NAMESAKE...

LEGEND HAS IT THAT CENTURIES AGO WHEN GOD THREW A TANTRUM AND FLOODED THE EARTH, TONANTZIN, IN AN ACT OF BOTH DEFIANCE AND COMPASSION, BREAST-FED THE SURVIVORS WITH PULQUE...

NOW, REMEMBER MY CHILDREN -- OH, JUST A SEC-- GOD! WHAT DID I TELL YOU ABOUT GOING NEAR THAT FAUCET AGAIN--?!?

A FEW YEARS BACK OUR OWN TONANTZIN STAYED UP FOR FORTY-TWO HOURS STRAIGHT PREPARING DOZENS OF BABOSAS FOR THE HOMELESS VICTIMS OF AN EARTHQUAKE THAT STRUCK THEIR FAR AWAY VILLAGE...

THEY'RE ALL YOURS, CARMEN!

OK, BOYS! LET'S LOAD 'EM UP! C'MON!

OUR TONANTZÍN IS ONLY AS MORTAL AS ANYONE, OF COURSE; BUT THERE ARE THOSE FELLOWS WHOLLY CONVINCED THAT AFTER EXPERIENCING BOTH HER SPLENDID COOKING TALENTS AND SEXUAL PROWESS IN BED, SHE AND HER DIVINE NAMESAKE CAN ONLY BE ONE AND THE SAME..!

--THEN THERE'S ALWAYS THE FOLKS WHO PREFER LIKENING HER TO THE DEVIL.

PLEASE, TONANTZIN!! THE HEAD SCISSORS NEXT! THE HEAD SCISSORS NEXT--

KRRRUNCH

BUT WE DIGRESS. BACK IN PALOMAR...

HERE YOU GO, THEO. THE FRUITS OF YOUR LABOR.

NO FRUIT! I WANT BABOSAS...

MAYBE I OUGHT TO STAY HERE TODAY HELPING YOU SELL THEM BOOGERS, HUH?

HO, YOU WISH! IF SHERIFF CHELO SAYS KIDS OVER SIX AND UNDER EIGHTEEN HAVE TO GO TO SCHOOL, THAT MEANS YOU, GIRLIE!

101

4

PULQUE- AN ALCOHOLIC DRINK HUMANS MAKE FROM THE MAGUEY PLANT

The Reticent Heart

The Reticent Heart

HELL, I CAN'T TELL HER ABOUT BEING JUMPED BY THAT PANTHER THE TIME ME AND THE GUYS HAD TO GO LOOKING FOR JESUS IN THE MOUNTAINS A FEW MONTHS AGO. JEEZ..!

SHE'D COMPLETELY FLIP OUT IF I TOLD HER! SHE'D--SHE'D--I DON'T WANT TO THINK ABOUT IT.

SHE THINKS I GOT THESE SCARS ON MY NECK AND SHOULDERS FROM FALLING INTO A BUSH.

SEE "THE LAUGHING SUN"-- BETO.

AT LEAST...THAT'S WHAT I HOPE SHE THINKS..!

HERACLIO, COME TO BED. YOU'VE GOT TO GO TO WORK-- OH. WRITING TO A SECRET ADMIRER?

I'M WRITING A LETTER TO JESUS. HAVEN'T FOR A WHILE...

I DON'T SUPPOSE HE GETS A LOT OF MAIL BEING STUCK IN THAT PRISON. BUT I DIDN'T KNOW HE COULD READ...

OH, IT'S SATCH AND ISRAEL YOU'RE THINKING OF. JESUS AND VICENTE CAN GET BY OK, BUT SATCH AND ISRAEL; I DUNNO, THEY'RE STUBBORN...

HERACLIO... AFTER WE WERE MARRIED...DID YOU HATE TEACHING ME TO READ..?

OH, CARMEN..! OF COURSE NOT. YOU WERE A WONDERFUL STUDENT. WHY?

BECAUSE I HATED EVERY SECOND OF IT.

DON'T STAY UP TOO LONG WITH THAT, OK?

Gilbert Hernandez

CARMEN'S LESS THAN SUBTLE HONESTY IS SOMETHING HERACLIO HAS LEARNED TO ADMIRE IN HIS WIFE,

BUT...

FATE HAS SEEN FIT TO BURDEN HERACLIO WITH CERTAIN EXPERIENCES HE PREFERS TO REVEAL TO NO ONE, FOR FEAR OF HURTING THOSE HE LOVES.

FLASHBACK: A FEW YEARS BEFORE CARMEN AND HERACLIO BECAME WIFE AND HUSBAND...

HEY KING DONG!

WELL, I WILL BE A SON OF A BITCH...

ALL RIGHT. WHERE'D YOU GUYS STEAL IT?

STEAL IT? HEY, MAN, I BOUGHT THIS BABY CASH MONEY!

NAW, REALLY. ISN'T THIS YOUR BOSS'S CAR, JESÚS? I REMEMBER YOU TELLING ME 'BOUT IT..

HE LET ME USE IT OVERNIGHT. C'MON, ISRAEL. WE'RE GOING TO SAN FIDEO. BABES, MAN.

SHIT, I WISH. I'LL BE FINISHED HERE BY MIDNIGHT IF I'M LUCKY. LOOK AT YOU GUYS! DRINKIN' BEERS IN BROAD DAYLIGHT! WOTTA WORLD!

HEY SATCH, VICENTE SAYS YOU'LL PISS YOUR PANTS FIRST GIRL YOU MEET!

FUK YEH...

TSCH!

3

DOWNTOWN SAN FIDEO AT NIGHT--!

FOR THE JADED; A SHIMMERING, SHALLOW PURGATORY...

TO THE RESTLESS YOUNG: AN OASIS AMID THE WASTELAND THEY FEEL IS THEIR LIVES...

Gilbert Hernandez

42

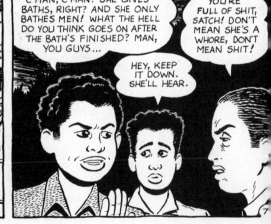

The Reticent Hear

BESIDES, ISRAEL'S GONE TO HER FOR BATHS BEFORE AND HE SAYS SHE DOESN'T. SAME WITH GABRIEL, LUTHER, THAT GUY WITH THE SIDEBURNS...

HEY, JESUS. IF YOU'RE SO GOD DAMN CRAZY ABOUT THE BROAD...

HOW COME YOU'VE NEVER GONE TO GET A BATH FROM HER?

SATCH... SATCH, YOU DON'T KNOW NOTHIN'!

THERE WASN'T A SNOWBALLS CHANCE IN HELL HERACLIO MIGHT REVEAL TO HIS FRIENDS THE NATURE OF THE RECOLLECTIONS RUNNING THROUGH HIS MIND JUST THEN. RECOLLECTIONS THAT BEGAN THE MOMENT THEY PICKED UP LUBA FROM THE GAS STATION.

AH~!
BUT THERE'S NO REASON WHY **YOU** SHOULDN'T KNOW JUST WHAT THOSE RECOLLECTIONS ARE:

*··· **FLASHBACK** WITHIN THE **FLASHBACK** ···*

YEARS AGO, ON A WARM, LATE AFTERNOON IN PALOMAR ...

MOM WANTS ME TO QUIT MY JOB PASSING OUT FLYERS FOR SEÑORA LUBA'S BATHING BUSINESS...

BUT HOW AM I GONNA TELL THE SEÑORA WITHOUT GETTING MY BLOCK KNOCKED OFF? THAT SEÑORA GETS MAD PRETTY EASY...

YO! I'M IN LUCK. HERE COMES HER COUSIN OFELIA. I'LL JUST TELL HER...

'SCUSE ME, SEÑORA, BUT ABOUT THIS JOB I HAVE WITH YOUR COUSIN...

TELL HER ABOUT IT! I CAN'T TALK TO HER WHEN SHE'S LIKE THIS!

COME ALONG, MARICELA.

ARGH... WELL, HERE GOES.

⑧

Gilbert Hernandez

45

The Reticent Heart

"I STAGGERED HOME WITH THE MIXED FEEL-INGS OF EXHILARATION AND CONFUSION NOT SETTING WELL IN MY BELLY. I LOVED THE EXPERIENCE ...AND I HATED IT.

MUMMY!

"IN THE MANY WEEKS THAT FOLLOWED, I DEVELOPED A REALLY BIG CRUSH ON HER, NATURALLY, BUT SHE NEVER LET ME NEAR HER AGAIN. I MEAN, WE SAID HI, BUT-- WELL, I EVENTUALLY GOT OVER HER WHEN SCHOOL STARTED...

"CAN YOU UNDERSTAND WHY I'VE NEVER TOLD ANY-ONE? IT WOULD HAVE GOTTEN AROUND TO JESUS EVENTUALLY FOR SURE! AND CARMEN! HAVING CAR-MEN FIND OUT WOULD BE WORSE THAN FACING A DOZEN ATTACKING PANTHERS! NO THANKS!"

I'M GOING TO MARRY CARMEN JIMENEZ. SHE MUST NEVER KNOW ABOUT THAT NIGHT.

I'M NOT IN THE HABIT OF RUINING REPUTATIONS ...

ESPECIALLY MY OWN!

NOW BACK TO OUR ORIGINAL FLASHBACK ...

SEE YOU GUYS LATER.

LATER, BOYOS.

LATER.

LATER.

THANKS A LOT, GUY. COME BY FOR A BATH SOME-TIME, HUH?

ALL RIGHT.

SO WHEN'S THE WEDDING, JESUS?

FUCK YOU.

Gilbert Hernandez

PRESENT TIME: MORNING COMES, AND IT'S OFF TO WORK FOR HERACLIO...

DON'T FORGET TO MAIL YOUR LETTER, SWEETHEART.

OK, QUERIDA.

G'MORNING, TONANTZIN. HI KIDS. HOW WAS TODAY'S HARVEST?

YOU'LL FIND OUT COME DINNERTIME, BOOGERFACE.

MORNING, SEÑORA.

GOOD MORNING, SEÑOR.

SAY, CHELO. EVER NOTICE HOW LUBA'S TEN YEAR OLD DAUGHTER LOOKS A LOT LIKE HERACLIO?

GUADALUPE? HM. MANUEL WAS HER FATHER. YOU REMEMBER; HE WAS KILLED...

MANUEL..? OH, YEAH! THAT GUY WAS A REAL LOVERBOY--!

HERACLIO WAS ONLY WHAT, FIFTEEN YEARS OLD THEN? I SERIOUSLY DOUBT THAT HE AND LUBA-- YOU KNOW...

BUT WOULDN'T IT BE A SCREAM IF THEY HAD?

THAT STUFF ONLY HAPPENS IN LITTLE BOYS' HEADS, CHELO.

END

48

THE WAY THINGS'RE GOING

BETO 85

VICENTE CAME HOME ONE DAY LOOKING PRETTY BEAT. HE HAD JUST LOST HIS JOB AT THE PLANT.

HE SAID THEY DIDN'T GIVE HIM ANY REASON FOR THE SACK AND WHEN HE WENT TO TALK TO ONE OF THE BOSSES, GATO, A GUY HE'S KNOWN FOR AT LEAST TWENTY YEARS, THE BUM SAYS "IT'S OUT OF MY HANDS." AND THAT WAS IT! LIKE KNOWING A GUY FOR TWENTY YEARS DOESN'T MEAN A GODDAMN THING! THEY WEREN'T BOSOM BUDDIES BUT THEY WEREN'T GODDAMN ENEMIES, EITHER!

I'D BEEN OUT OF A JOB MYSELF FOR THREE WEEKS WITH NO PROSPECTS IN SIGHT. I WAS ALREADY DOWN TO MY LAST FEW BUCKS AND MOST OF VICENTE'S LAST CHECK WENT TO PAYING OFF HIS DEBTS. DON'T EVEN MENTION WOMEN...

I FORGET WHY, BUT WE GOT INTO A FIST FIGHT. I BUST TWO KNUCKLES 'CAUSE THAT RIGHT SIDE OF HIS FACE IS PRETTY TOUGH. HE WALKS OUT WITH ONLY A POPPED LIP.

VICENTE COMES BACK WITH A BOTTLE OF CHEAP WINE AND WE'RE PALS AGAIN.

Gilbert Hernandez

WE PUT ON OUR GOOD SUITS AND HIT DOWNTOWN. INSTEAD OF JOBS FALLING INTO OUR LAPS, WE FIND OURSELVES IN THE MIDST OF DOZENS OF *PEOPLES* IN *THEIR* GOOD SUITS WITH THE SAME LOOK ON THEIR FACES THAT I'VE BEEN SEEING IN THE MIRROR LATELY.

WE MUST HAVE COVERED THIRTY PLACES THAT DAY. EVERYWHERE WE WENT THERE MUST HAVE BEEN AT LEAST TWENTY GUYS AHEAD OF US. CONSTRUCTION JOBS, CARWASHES, DISHWASHERS, EVEN THE LOWEST SHIT JOBS WERE TAKEN; THE JOBS ONLY THE POOREST OF THE POOR LOCAL INDIANS USUALLY ACCEPT. VICENTE AND I CONSIDER BECOMING HOUSEWIVES.

LATER WE MEET UP WITH A FRIEND OF VICENTE'S FROM PALOMAR NAMED LUBA. I DON'T USUALLY GET ALONG WITH THEM INDIANS FROM UP NORTH, BUT SHE'S O.K; SHE'S NOT STUCK UP LIKE MOST OF HER PEOPLE.

WHILE THEY SHOOT THE SHIT I STEP OVER TO THE CURB TO SCRAPE OFF SOME DRIED DOGSHIT FROM MY HEEL. THIS LADY PASSING BY LOOKS AT VICENTE AND LUBA AND CRACKS TO HER FRIEND, "NOW AREN'T *THEY* A PAIR..."

VICENTE AND LUBA OVERHEAR THIS AND THEY FIGURE THE BITCH WAS REFERRING TO VICENTE'S MISMATCHED SHOES. HE WAS HOPING NO ONE'D NOTICE THAT HE HAD DYED A BROWN RIGHT SHOE TO MATCH HIS BLACK LEFT ONE.

AFTER LUBA'S GONE VICENTE TELLS ME HE DIDN'T MENTION TO HER OUR SORRY SITUATION EVEN THOUGH HE WAS SURE SHE WOULD'VE BEEN GLAD TO HELP US OUT MONEYWISE. PRIDE. IT'LL KILL YOU, I'M TELLING YOU.

THAT NIGHT AT HOME I MAKE MY USUAL SOUNDS ABOUT JOINING THE ARMY AND ONCE AGAIN VICENTE TALKS ME OUT OF IT...

The Reticent Heart

VICENTE FIGURES WE'LL BE FIGHTING THE U.S. FOR SOME REASON OR ANOTHER SOONER OR LATER. HE'S PROBABLY RIGHT, THE WAY THINGS ARE GOING...

AS I DRIFTED OFF TO SLEEP I RECALLED SOME PARTICULAR NEWS FROM THE U.S. I'D HEARD THAT DAY: A MARRIED MAN AND WOMAN WERE ATTACKED ON THE STREET BY TEENAGED BOYS WHO MISTOOK THE WOMAN FOR A GUY. UH...DID THOSE GUYS EXPECT TO KILL THAT COUPLE, BECAUSE THEY DIDN'T; OR DID THEY THINK A BLACK EYE OR A BUSTED ARM WILL PREVENT THE SPREAD OF A.I.D.S..?

YEAH, WELL, THE WAY THINGS ARE GOING THE EARTH OUGHT TO BE ASSUMED FLAT AGAIN IN A FEW YEARS...

I HAVE THIS DREAM AND VICENTE'S FRIEND LUBA'S IN IT. SHE'S FALLEN INTO THIS DEEP HOLE AND I'M RUNNING AROUND TRYING TO FIND HER SOMETHING TO EAT. I DON'T UNDERSTAND DREAMS MYSELF...

A WEEK PASSES AND OUR LUCK REMAINS PATHETIC. WE'RE DOWN TO ONE MEAL A DAY. RICE AND COCA COLA. THE MUTTS IN OUR NEIGHBORHOOD BEGIN TO LOOK TASTY. WELL, ALMOST.

I WAKE UP ONE MORNING AND VICENTE'S ALREADY GONE. YOUR CHANCES OF BEING HIRED SOMEWHERE ARE BETTER IF YOU'RE ALONE ANYWAY, SO I GET DRESSED AND I'M OUT THERE.

FUCKING BROAD DAYLIGHT AND THESE KIDS JUMP ME AND STEAL MY COAT AND WHAT'S LEFT OF MY MONEY.

I SAT THERE BOTH LAUGHING AND CRYING. I SHOULD HAVE SOLD THE COAT MYSELF FOR EXTRA CASH LIKE I HAD PLANNED BEFORE.

FOR A DELIRIOUS MOMENT I THOUGHT OF GOING BACK TO MY WIFE, BUT I CAME TO MY SENSES BEFORE I EVEN SCRAPED MYSELF UP OFF THE DIRT.

I WENT HOME TO GET MY NOT-SO-GOOD COAT AND SET OFF AGAIN. I DIDN'T WANT TO GIVE MYSELF ANY TIME TO SIT AROUND THE HOUSE TO MOPE IN SELF-PITY.

③

Gilbert Hernandez

BY MIDDAY I WAS FEELING SHITTY; MY SIDES HURT FROM THOSE KIDS' GOD DAMN HARD SHOES, I WAS FAMISHED AND A GORGEOUS NUBIAN MAIDEN CAUGHT ME PICKING MY NOSE.

I SLIP INTO AN ALLEY TO SPIT UP IN PRIVATE WHEN THIS GUY IN A SHARP SUIT COMES OUT OF THE BACK DOOR OF THIS DINKY RESTAURANT AND HE ASKS ME IF I WANT A JOB. I ALMOST SHIT. IT'S ONLY A LOWLIFE BUS BOY DEAL, BUT THE WAY THINGS ARE GOING ...

WE WALK INTO THE SMALL SMELLY KITCHEN AND I MEET THE COOK. I MANAGE TO TALK 'EM INTO A QUICK MEAL THAT THEY DEDUCT FROM MY PAY. WELL, I TOOK ONE BITE AND WAS OUT OF THERE LIKE A FLASH.

I WALKED FAST BECAUSE I DIDN'T WANT TO GIVE MYSELF ENOUGH TIME TO CHANGE MY MIND OUT OF DESPERATION. OR OUT OF SENSE. THE FASTER I WALKED THE MORE ANGRY I GOT. WAS I ANGRY..!

THAT ASSHOLE IN THE SHARP SUIT TELLS ME THAT ANOTHER GUY HAD BEEN IN EARLIER FOR THE JOB BUT THEY DIDN'T HIRE HIM BECAUSE HALF HIS FACE WAS FUCKED UP AND HE MIGHT HAVE KEPT CUSTOMERS AWAY. THEY TOLD HIM IT WAS BECAUSE OF HIS EARRING. AND KNOWING THAT DAMN VICENTE HE PROBABLY BELIEVED 'EM!

I FOUND VICENTE AT HOME BUSILY PREPARING A STEAK DINNER FOR THE BOTH OF US. TWO BOTTLES OF COLD GERMAN BEER AWAITED OUR PARCHED PALATES. HIS GOOD SUIT COAT WAS NOWHERE TO BE SEEN.

PRIDE. IT'LL KILL YOU, I'M TELLING YOU.

The Reticent Hear

Gilbert Hernandez

The Reticent Heart

Gilbert Hernandez

The Reticent Heart

IT'S ABOUT US, CARMEN. IT'S ABOUT OUR LIVES, UH...WELL, NOT *OUR* LIVES, BUT-- OK, THIS:

REBECA BUENDÍA GOT UP AT THREE IN THE MORNING WHEN SHE LEARNED THAT AURELIANO WOULD BE SHOT.

SHE STAYED IN THE BEDROOM IN THE DARK, WATCHING THE CEMETERY WALL THROUGH THE HALF-OPENED WINDOW AS THE BED ON WHICH SHE SAT SHOOK WITH JOSÉ ARCADIO'S SNORING.

IF YOU SAY SO, SWEETHEART.

OK, CLASS. THAT'LL BE IT FOR TODAY.

PRACTICE THOSE CHORDS, YSLAS.

HEY, PROFESOR! EVEN A MUSIC TEACHER NEEDS A DRINK NOW AND THEN!

OH, GLORIA, THANKS, BUT I DON'T WANT TO MISS THE BUS...

I'LL DRIVE YOU HOME, SILLY. HERACLIO, IF YOU DON'T LOOSEN UP YOU'RE GOING TO WIND UP LOOKING LIKE THAT *MUNCH* PRINT.

THAT BAD, HUH? *HEH.* MY WIFE MADE ME TAKE IT OUT OF THE HOUSE BECAUSE A GUEST MIGHT THINK THEIR HOSTS HAD PAINT-ED SUCH A THING.

ACTUALLY, *I'M* THE ONE WHO SOMETIMES FEELS THAT WAY WHEN I'M TEACHING MY GRAMMAR CLASS.

WHAT'S THE POINT?

WHO EVER *REALLY* LEARNS ANYTHING?

EEAAAUUURRRGH...

Gilbert Hernandez

The Reticent Hear

Gilbert Hernandez

The Reticent Heart

DIDN'T REALIZE IT WAS SO LATE-- WHOOP...MAYBE SHE'LL BE ASLEEP AN' I CAN SNEAK IN--

WHAT AM I SAYING?! WHO IS SHE? MY MOTHER?!

SHE'S STILL UP...GOT YOUR ROLLING PIN OUT, EH SHORTY? WELL, I SAY *PHOOEY!*

..I WON'T GIVE HER THE SATISFACTION! GOTTA MAKE HER UNDERSTAND SHE CAN'T SHOVE ME AROUND...! THINKS I'M A WIMP, EH? HAH, I'D LOOK UP OL' GLORIA IF SHE DIDN'T LIVE TWO TOWNS AWAY!

I KNOW... *LA INDIA.* YEAH, LUBA'S ALWAYS BEEN A PAL TO ME. CARMEN STILL DOESN'T KNOW THAT LUBA TOOK MY VIRGINITY YEARS AGO. IN FACT, NOBODY KNOWS BUT ME AND OL' LUBE...

HELL, YEAH...I'LL GIVE CARMEN SOMETHING TO BE MAD ABOUT NOW...!

MOM, THERE'S SOMEONE OUT THERE...!

OH, IT'S NOTHING, KIDS. GO ON BACK TO BED NOW.

I'M READY FOR HIM, LUBA!

OH, OFELIA! PUT THAT AWAY! I KNOW WHO IT IS!

SUMP SUMP

Gilbert Hernandez

63

SEE HERE NOW...

ZIP!
ZIP!

FUD

IS HE HURT?

NO, YOU GO TO BED. I'LL TAKE CARE OF THIS.

WHAT A PAL WHAT A PAL WHAT A PAL...

AND WITH PALS LIKE YOU, WHO NEEDS A WIFE, EH..?

MUA!

YOU WOULDN'T CLOBBER ME WITH A BOWL OF HOT SOUP, WOULD YOU PAL!?!

NO, BUT THE MERE THOUGHT MAKES MY MOUTH WATER...

GOOD OL' LUBA...YOU'VE PROBABLY TAKEN MORE SHIT THAN ANYBODY IN THIS GODDAMN TOWN OF NEANDERTHALS! GUYS ALWAYS BUGGING YOU AND SHIT, WOMEN WITH THEIR DAMN GOSSIP..

YOU'VE GOT MORE GUTS AND TOLERANCE OF ANYONE I KNOW, LUBA. WHY DO YOU STAY IN PALOMAR? WHAT'S IN IT FOR YOU..?

MMHMM...

SIGH, I'M HERE BECAUSE OF MY WIFE CARMEN...SHE LOVES THIS TOWN, THE PEOPLE..WELL, NOT EVERYBODY. SHE'S NOT TOO CRAZY ABOUT YOU, Y'KNOW...

A FRIEND TRIED TO TELL ME THAT WAS BECAUSE CARMEN AND I HAVEN'T BEEN ABLE TO HAVE KIDS AND YOU'RE NOT MARRIED AND YOU'VE GOT FOUR GIRLS RUNNING AROUND. I DUNNO, CARMEN WON'T SAY ANYTHING...

MAN, CAN SHE BE UNREASONABLE! IF SHE *KNEW* ABOUT THAT NIGHT YEARS AGO WHEN YOU AND ME... JEEZ...

LUBA HAD ALMOST FORGOTTEN ABOUT THAT ENCOUNTER. IT WAS SUCH A TRIVIAL MATTER TO HER THEN THAT SHE WAS NOT CERTAIN WHICH OF THE BOYS SHE HAD SEDUCED THAT NIGHT...

HEY, LUBA...ABOUT THAT NIGHT..? WHY... HOW COME? I MEAN, I WAS JUST A DUMB KID, I DIDN'T... WHY? WHAT WAS IN IT FOR YOU..?

The Reticent Heart

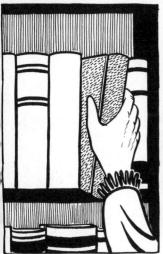

"UR-URSULA..SAW....PRU-DEN-CIO...AG-UI-- AGUILAR..AGAIN....IN..THE..BATHROOM...UM, US-ING....THE..ES-ES-PAR-TO..PLUG..TO..WASH THE..CLOT-TED..BLOOD..FROM ...HIS..TH-TH··"

WHO'S THERE..? CARMEN? WHAT'S WRONG?

OH. OK, C'MON IN.

The Reticent Hea

Gilbert Hernandez

AN AMERICAN IN PALOMAR

ARE YOU ALL RIGHT, SEÑORITA?

Y-YES, THANK YOU, SEÑOR.

HOW MUCH?

UH...UH, SIX FOR ONE, EIGHT FOR TWO..?

= BETO·85

BYE.

GOOD DAY.

COPY RIGHT © GILBERT HERNANDEZ 1985

--AND HE EVEN BOUGHT A BABOSA THAT FELL IN THE DIRT !!!

I'M GOING TO KILL THAT AUGUSTÍN! I DON'T KNOW WHAT GETS OVER HIM.

OH, IT'S CLEAR TO ME HE BUGS TONANTZÍN BECAUSE HE LIKES HER, CARMEN.

The Reticent Hea

YEAH, WELL, MY FIST LIKES HIS EYEBALL QUITE A BIT, TOO, SO...

AS FOR YOUR WHITE KNIGHT, TONANTZÍN; HE'S A PHOTOGRAPHER FROM THE STATES AND HE TELLS ME HE'S USING OUR TOWN AS THE SUBJECT OF A PICTURE BOOK HE HOPES TO PUBLISH...

HE'S ALREADY, EH, TAKEN QUITE A FEW PICTURES OF ME, AHEM...

OH, REALLY! I SUPPOSE HE TOLD YOU HE WAS A HOLLYWOOD PHOTOGRAPHER AND YOU'RE HIS LATEST FIND!

SMICK SMOCK...

CLOSE ENOUGH, SMARTY. HE'S PHOTOGRAPHED EVERYTHING FROM FASHION MODELS TO TRAIN WRECKS TO WEDDINGS. HE TOLD ME I WAS MORE EXCITING TO PHOTOGRAPH THAN ANY NUDE HE'S EVER HAD TO DO! SMICK SMOCK...

TSK TSK. I ALWAYS SAID GRINGOS WERE CRAZY.

WELL, I KNOW WHERE TO FIND HIM IF HE GETS OUT OF LINE WITH HIS SNOOPING. HE'S RENTING SEÑOR TA-TA'S OLD PLACE.

HOLLY WOOD--?

CLICK!

WHAT IS PLAYING, SEÑORA?

JERRY LEWIS. I ORDER BRUCE LEE AND THEY SEND ME JERRY LEWIS.

YUK.

CINEM

LUCHA LIBRE

KILLER CAROL KOVNICK vs LILIAN LUST

3

Gilbert Hernandez

69

AS FAR AS HOLLYWOOD MOVIES GO, MY FAVORITES ARE THE OLD ONES; YOU KNOW, MOVIES WITH JIMMY CAGNEY, JEAN ARTHUR, MONTGOMERY CLIFT...

NOT TOO MANY PEOPLE SHOW UP FOR THE MOVIES I LIKE, BUT I'LL TELL YOU, THE PLACE IS ALWAYS PACKED FOR BRUCE LEE OR ELVIS PRESLEY. I THOUGHT THERE'D BE A RIOT WHEN I RAN 'VIVA LAS VEGAS'...

HEY, WOULD YOU KNOW WHY I CAN'T FIND ANY NEW BRUCE LEE MOVIES ANYMORE? HE SEEMED TOO YOUNG TO RETIRE.

BRUCE LEE DIED SEVERAL YEARS AGO. I DO NOT REMEMBER HOW IT HAPPENED, THOUGH.

OH.

HM. HE WAS SO CUTE, TOO, TSK...

HELL, I THINK WE'D BETTER KEEP THAT TO OURSELVES. IF ANYBODY AROUND HERE HEARS THAT-- WHOOSH!

SEÑORA, MAY I TAKE A FEW PICTURES OF YOU AND YOUR GIRLS HERE IN FRONT OF THE THEATER?

OH! WELL...!

I'LL TELL YOU WHAT. MY TWO OLDER GIRLS ARE IN SCHOOL RIGHT NOW, BUT TOMORROW'S SATURDAY...

WELL, HOW ABOUT TOMORROW AT NOON, WITH YOUR WHOLE FAMILY THEN?

UM... FINE.

THAT'LL GIVE ME TIME TO GET MY GIRLS ALL DRESSED UP NICE. NOT TO MENTION MYSELF. AH, NOW WE'LL HAVE A NICE PICTURE TO SEND TO RELATIVES.

HMMMMM

'NICE' PICTURES ARE THE LAST THING HOWARD MILLER WANTS FROM HIS VISIT TO PALOMAR.

NO 'HOT' PHOTOJOURNALIST EVER GOT THE NOTORIETY MILLER SEEKS SHOOTING SUNSETS AND WATERFALLS.

The Reticent Hea

THE MORE TRAGIC, HUMOROUS, SENTIMENTAL OR WRETCHED THE BETTER FOR MILLER, AS HE HAS FOUND IN THE PEOPLE OF PALOMAR THE IDEAL SUBJECT MATTER FOR THE BOOK HE HOPES WILL ESTABLISH HIS (SELF-PROCLAIMED) GENIUS TO THE ART WORLD...

WITH YEARS OF EXPERIENCE FREELANCING FOR VARIOUS GEOGRAPHIC MAGAZINES BEHIND HIM, HOWARD MILLER IS FAMILIAR WITH HIS CHOSEN SOURCE MATERIAL WHILE JADED BY IT AS WELL...

JUST ANOTHER GROUP OF INDIANS AND BLACKS AND WHATEVERS TO HIM...

HE BELIEVES IT IS HIS 'AESTHETIC GENIUS', HOWEVER, THAT WILL MAKE ALL THE DIFFERENCE.

AS FOR FRATERNIZING WITH THE NATIVES, MILLER HAS FOUND THEM TO BE QUAINTLY CONVIVIAL, IF SOME OF THEM PERHAPS TOO FRIENDLY...

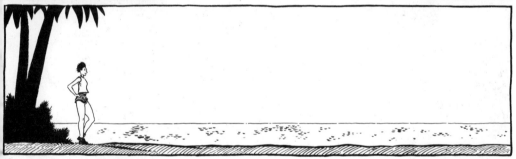

Gilbert Hernandez

HO!

HO!

HO YOURSELF! HOW'D I DO?

HUFF HUFF

10.94 FOR 100 METERS IS REALLY QUITE GOOD, DIANA!

⟨WISH I WAS SURE WHAT THE WORLD RECORD IS...⟩

LET ME DO IT AGAIN! ONCE MORE!

ROWR!

AS OF THIS TIME, EVELYN ASHFORD HELD THE RECORD AT 10.76 FOR 100 METERS/ 8.23.84

READY?

SET?

GO!

GO! GO! GO!

CLICK

YOW! ALMOST LOST MY HEAD FOR A SECOND--!!

HUFF HUFF

9.98!

⟨HOLD ON! THAT CAN'T BE RIGHT! THAT'S WAY PASSED THE WORLD RECORD!⟩

DIANA! ONCE MORE! I WANT TO BE SURE!

10.97! STILL REMARKABLE! DIANA, IF THAT PREVIOUS TIME IS CORRECT... THEN YOU HAVE MOST LIKELY BEAT THE OUTDOORS WORLD RECORD FOR WOMEN EASILY!

I'M THE FASTEST GIRL IN THE WORLD!

NO YOU'RE NOT, DIANA, 'CAUSE YOUR SISTER TONANTZIN CAN CATCH YOU ANY OL' TIME!

REALLY?

⟨MY WATCH MUST BE WRONG. IT MUST BE-⟩

⟨AMERICAN ENGLISH⟩

FOR YEARS HOWARD MILLER HAS ENTERTAINED HIS OWN THEORY THAT THE *TRULY* GREAT ATHLETES OF THE WORLD NEVER ENTER OR NEVER MAKE IT TO THOSE SPORTING EVENTS DESIGNED TO DETERMINE WORLD RECORDS AND SUCH...

MILLER CERTAINLY NEVER EXPECTED TO HAVE HIS MUSINGS CONFIRMED IN PALOMAR...!

6

The Reticent Heart

Gilbert Hernandez

<FUCKING AMAZING. I'M NOT SURE ANYBODY IN THE STATES KNOWS ABOUT THIS PLACE.>

<I'LL HAVE TO COME BACK WITH A FLASH-LIGHT AND MAYBE A GUIDE.>

<HOLD IT... I JUST CAME IN THIS WAY... OR WAS IT--?>

<WAIT A MINUTE. I DIDN'T COME IN THAT FAR! WHERE THE HELL IS THAT SUNLIGHT?!>

<I DON'T BELIEVE THIS! HOW DID I--?>

HEY, THEO! THEO, CAN YOU HEAR ME?!

The Reticent Hear

AN
AMERICAN
IN PALOMAR

TO BE
CONCLUDED
IN PART
TWO

The Reticent Hear

THE DAY BEFORE, THAT MAN FROM
THE UNITED STATES TOLD HER SHE WAS
POSSIBLY THE FASTEST WOMAN
SPRINTER IN THE WORLD...

THIS IS THE REASON DIANA VILLASEÑOR
IS UP SO EARLY ON A SATURDAY MORNING,
A DAY WHEN HER OLDER SISTER TONANTZÍN
USUALLY ALLOWS HER TO SLEEP IN.

UP UNTIL LAST NIGHT, THE
ONLY ACTIVITY DIANA LOVED
MORE THAN RUNNING WAS
SLEEPING. THAT HAS NOW
CHANGED.

THE FASTEST WOMAN
IN THE WORLD.

THE PROSPECT OF THAT SENT
DIANA'S IMAGINATION SOARING.
SHE FANCIED THE ROAR OF CROWDS
AS SHE WINS EVERY RACE, THE KISSES
OF HANDSOME CHAMPION ATHLETES,
AND OF BEING THE FIRST WOMAN
ON MARS.

THEN, THE INEVITABLE LOW
AFTER THE HIGH.

EXISTENTIAL CONTEMPLATION
KEPT HER AWAKE MOST OF THE NIGHT,
WHEN FINALLY SHE CAME TO A
CONCLUSION:

DIANA HAS DECIDED
NOW SHE MUST BE THE
FASTEST OF ALL.

Gilbert Hernandez

The Reticent Heart

Gilberto Hernandez

IT IS SO NICE THAT GOD HAS SEEN FIT TO GIVE YOU SUCH BEAUTIFUL CURLY HAIR, DORALIS, AND NOT THAT MATTED NIGHTMARE THAT GROWS FROM YOUR MOTHER'S HEAD.

HUH. THE POT CALLS THE KETTLE BLACK...

HOLD STILL, CASIMIRA.

MOM, IS IT TRUE WHITE PEOPLE COPY EVERYTHING THEY KNOW FROM NORMAL PEOPLE?

GUADALUPE! NO! WHO TOLD YOU THAT!?

NO, SWEETHEART, BUT THEY DANCE LIKE THEY'VE GOT WEBBED FEET, HUH, OFELIA?

DA!

LUBA, THAT'S ENOUGH!

YOUR MOTHER'S TALKING SILLY, GIRLS. SHE USED TO GO OUT WITH THIS ONE WHITE GUY YEARS AGO...

MMMMM, YEAH. BUT THAT GRIGORYEVICH ARTZYBASCHEV WAS A LIVING DOLL!

WHERE'S THIS WHITE MAN GOING TO TAKE OUR PICTURE AT, MOM?

OH, MARICELA, THAT'S RIGHT! HE WANTED US IN FRONT OF THE MOVIE HOUSE! TSK, I'LL TELL YOU GUYS WHAT--

YOU GIRLS FIX UP THE LIVING ROOM A LITTLE BIT, AND I'LL BRING HIM OVER HERE.

OK, LET'S GO, GUYS...

INDEED, A PORTRAIT OF LUBA AND HER FAMILY IS WHAT MILLER WANTS FOR HIS BOOK, BUT IT IS NOT QUITE THE PICTURE LUBA IS EXPECTING...

TOMORROW AT NOON, THEN?

FINE.

GREAT! HOPE THE REST OF HER FAMILY LOOKS AS BEAT!

5

Gilbert Hernandez

81

MMMMM... GLAD TO SEE YOU'VE GOTTEN BACK TO SERIOUS BUSINESS, KID.

HOWARD AND I'VE BEEN BUSY BUSY BUSY, CARMEN. MODELING TAKES LONGER THAN YOU THINK, BUT HE'S A GENIUS SO IT WAS PRETTY EASY.

SO I HEAR. I ALSO HEARD SOME STUPID RUMOR THAT YOU WERE GONNA LEAVE WITH HIM TO THE STATES.

YEAH, SURE, I SAID, AND I SUPPOSE YOUR SISTER DIANA'S GONNA STAY RIGHT HERE BY HERSELF, WHILE··

WELL, I'M TAKING HER WITH US...

WHO KNOWS? MAYBE DIANA CAN GET A JOB AS AN ACTRESS OR SOMETHING HERSELF. I HEAR MOST FOLKS IN HOLLYWOOD SPEAK SPANISH ANYWAY, SO WE SHOULDN'T NEED HOWARD FOR TOO LONG; HE'S NICE, BUT, YOU KNOW...

NOW SCOOT, SHORTY. I'VE GOT TO FINISH HERE BEFORE DIANA GETS HOME. THIS BATCH OF BABOSAS MAY BE MY LAST.

TONANTZIN'S PROBABLY MY BEST FRIEND AND I LOVE HER, BUT SOMETIMES SHE GETS THE WRONG IDEA ABOUT THINGS...

SHE'S NEVER SHOVED ME OUT OF HER HOUSE BEFORE...

I'D BETTER TALK TO THIS GRINGO MYSELF...

NEVER CALLED ME SHORTY BEFORE, EITHER...

WHILE IT IS EVIDENT TONANTZIN KNOWS LITTLE OF THE WAYS OF THE WORLD OUTSIDE PALOMAR, PERHAPS LUBA KNOWS TOO MUCH...

SEÑOR MEELER.

〈EGAD!〉

CIR

The Reticent Hear

Gilbert Hernandez

<"GREAT SPIRITS HAVE ALWAYS ENCOUNTERED VIOLENT OPPOSITION FROM MEDIOCRE MINDS.">

<THAT'S WHAT EINSTEIN SAID, WOMAN! CHEW ON THAT A SPELL!>

HEY!

WAIT, WHAT..? SHE THINKS SHE IS COMING WITH ME--? WHATEVER GAVE HER THAT IDEA..?

OH, I CAN GUESS! NOW, IF YOU DON'T TALK TO HER SOON--

<DAMN! OF ALL THE GIRLS TO GET INVOLVED WITH, I WIND UP WITH A GODDAMN GROUPIE!>

WELL, IF I DON'T LOOK AFTER TONANTZIN, WHO WILL?

TONANTZIN! DON'T KEEP ME IN SUSPENSE! WHAT SURPRISE?! WHAT?!

DIANA, YOU'LL HAVE TO BE PATIENT. HOWARD WILL TELL YOU HIMSELF.

<CHRIST, THAT LUBA AND TONANTZIN GIVE NAIVETÉ A BAD NAME.>

<AH, BUT I SHOULDN'T BE ANGRY. I SUPPOSE BEING STUCK FOREVER IN A PLACE LIKE THIS WOULD IMPOVERISH ANYBODY'S LIFE. SAD...>

<WELL, THE MOST BEAUTIFUL FLOWERS GROW FROM SHIT, SO MY BOOK WILL BE ONE GROUNDBREAKING BOUQUET. HEY. I MAY HAVE A TITLE THERE.>

<SIGH, TONANTZIN, TSK... WHAT WILL I TELL HER?>

<GUESS I SIMPLY TELL HER THE TRUTH: I'M COMMITTED TO MY WORK; TO OTHER PEOPLE· I'LL SIMPLY TELL HER...>

8

The Reticent Hear

LIES. LIES ABOUT HIS EDITOR SENDING HIM ON ASSIGNMENT TO RUSSIA FOR TWO YEARS AND OTHER NONSENSE. HE DOESN'T KNOW WHEN HE WILL RETURN TO THE STATES BUT ISN'T IT WONDERFUL?

THAT'S...THE SURPRISE YOU TWO HAD FOR ME?

SURPRISE... OH. OH! YES, DIANA, SURPRISE! MY STOPWATCH WAS CORRECT AFTER ALL.

REALLY..? THEN... I AM THE FASTEST GIRL... OF ALL?

〈CHRIST. DID I REALLY SAY ALL THAT?〉

WOW!

TONANTZÍN...

〈SHUT UP, MILLER. JUST DON'T MOVE OR SAY ANYTHING.〉

⑨

Gilbert Hernandez

85

The Reticent Hear

...WINNER OF THE **KOVINICK PRIZE** FOR PHOTOJOURNALISM --**HOWARD MILLER!**

THANK YOU-- THANK YOU

I WOULD LIKE TO THANK ABSOLUTELY NO ONE FROM PALOMAR FOR THIS PRESTIGIOUS AWARD, AS IT WAS ONLY THROUGH MY EXTRAORDINARY AESTHETIC EYE THAT FINE ART COULD BE CULLED FROM SUCH AN OTHERWISE DREARY, OVERUSED SUBJECT...

TO MY ARTISTIC PEERS MORE FASCINATED WITH MY SUBJECT, I SAY VISIT PALOMAR AT YOUR OWN RISK. I CAN'T GUARANTEE YOU'LL ALSO EXPERIENCE THERE THE KIND OF PHYSICAL AND EMOTIONAL PAIN THAT BEGETS ART, BUT THE FOOD AND MUSIC MAY BE ENOUGH FOR YOU...

--AND BY NO MEANS FORGET OL' SEÑOR ALBERTO EINSTEIN'S GREAT QUOTE: "GREAT SPIRITS HAVE ALWAYS ENCOUNTERED VIOLENT OPPOSITION FROM MEDIOCRE MINDS"...

--BECAUSE THE MEDIOCRE MIND YOU ENCOUNTER MAY BE YOUR OWN.

WEEKS LATER, CARMEN WILL STILL NOT SPEAK TO SHERIFF CHELO FOR BREAKING AUGUSTIN'S ARM WHEN SHE ARRESTED HIM AND HIS GOONS FOR THE ASSAULT.

AS FOR THE BATTERED BUT WISER MILLER, HE GLADLY FOLLOWED CHELO'S SUGGESTION OF LEAVING PALOMAR WITHOUT SO MUCH AS A GOODBYE TO ANYONE.

SEE? I TOLD YOU!

YEAH, THEY'RE GRINGOS, ALL RIGHT. WONDER WHAT THEY'RE DOING?

WE SHOULD ASK 'EM IF THEY KNOW SEÑOR MEELER!

A LOT OF GRINGOS HAVE BEEN COMING AND GOING SINCE HE LEFT. WONDER IF HIS BOOK ABOUT US IS OUT ALREADY?

HMF.

THEN THEY'D KNOW THAT YOU'RE THE FASTEST GIRL IN THE WORLD, DIANA!

THEO, WHEN I'M THROUGH, I'M GONNA BE THE FASTEST EVER!

ARE YOU STILL HANGING ON TO THAT BULLSHIT?!

BULL--?

BULLSHIT! ALL THAT CRAP ABOUT WORLD RECORDS AND ART AND HOLLYWOOD! HE WAS A GENIUS, ALL RIGHT. GENIUS BULLSHITTER.

C'MON. LET'S GET TO WORK.

I AM THE FASTEST!

DIANA--!

I AM --- I AM--!

13

Gilbert Hernandez

89

DESPITE THE LOOKS OF THINGS, TONANTZIN HATED TO DO WHAT SHE JUST DID, BUT FEELS SHE HAD NO OTHER CHOICE: IF SHE DOESN'T LOOK AFTER DIANA, WHO WILL?

C'MON. LET'S GET TO WORK.

OF COURSE, TONANTZIN'S LITTLE DISPLAY HAS ONLY SERVED TO ENCOURAGE DIANA EVEN MORE.

TONANTZIN SAYS THAT SHE DOESN'T MISS MEELER MUCH, AS SHE NEVER HAD ANY REAL FEELINGS FOR HIM. SHE JUST WISHES HE'D HAVE BEEN AROUND TO PAY HALF THE ABORTION FEE.

I'M HOPING HER ENCOUNTER WITH HIM HAS ONCE AND FOR ALL EXORCISED HER NAIVE ASPIRATIONS OF CONQUERING SHOWBIZ.

BUT WE SHALL SEE WHAT WE SHALL SEE.

AS TIME PASSES IN PALOMAR, THE DAILY RITUALS OF WORK AND PLAY EASE THE MEMORY OF HOWARD MILLER AND HIS PROPOSED BOOK OUT OF THE MINDS OF THE PEOPLE. MOST FOLKS HAVE ALREADY FORGOTTEN HIS NAME, MUCH LESS REMEMBER HIS FACE.

BACK IN THE UNITED STATES MILLER WISHES HE COULD BE SO LUCKY.

The Reticent Hea

Gilbert Hernandez

holidays in the Sun

BETO SEPT. OCT. 85

2

JESÚS, IT'S OBREGON. HE'S GONNA DO IT THIS TIME, I THINK. WE TRIED TO STOP HIM.

SO WHAT MAKES YOU THINK I CAN--

AH. OK, SHIT.

HE'LL LISTEN TO YOU, MAN. HE'S ALWAYS SAYING HOW IT'S HIS FAULT YOU'RE HERE IN THE FIRST PLACE.

YEAH.

SHINK SHINK SHINK SHINK SHINK

OBREGON!

FORGET IT, JESUS! I'M GOING! YOU CAN'T STOP ME! I KNOW WHAT I'M DOING!

YOU'LL NEVER MAKE IT, OBREGON. WE'RE TOO FAR FROM THE MAINLAND. BESIDES, THE SHARKS...

SHARKS?! YOU THINK I'M SCARED OF SHARKS?! THE CRITTERS COULDN'T FINISH ME OFF THE FIRST TIME! I CAN HANDLE 'EM --

YOU'VE ONLY GOT TWENTY SIX MONTHS TO GO, FOOL! DON'T FUCK IT UP NOW--!

3

Ibert Hernandez

93

The Reticent Heart

THOUGH JESÚS ANGEL HAS NEVER HAD RELATIONS WITH LUBA, HE HAS INDEED INDULGED IN OVER FIFTEEN THOUSAND DIFFERENT SEXUAL FANTASIES OF THE WOMAN FROM THE MOMENT HE FIRST SET HIS EYES ON HER SOME TWELVE YEARS AGO IN PALOMAR...

NOW, TO JESÚS'S CONFUSION, HIS ESTRANGED WIFE LAURA IS REPLACING LUBA MIDWAY THROUGH THESE IMAGINARY INTERLUDES.

BUT WHY? LAURA IS THE LAST PERSON HE WANTS TO THINK ABOUT...

I'M TELLING YOU, JESÚS, THAT DROMUNDO DOESN'T SCARE ME ONE BIT!

YEAH, HE'S UP THERE ON THE HILL EVERYDAY LOOKING DOWN ON US, BUT HE WON'T COME DOWN HERE, NO SIR..!

I GOT A PLAN THAT EVEN HE CAN'T STOP, MAN! IF YOU WANT IN ON IT JUST LET ME KNOW, HUH..?

♪ JESUS ♪

6

The Reticent Heart

THE HELL WITH THAT NOISE, BOY! C'MON IN! THE WATER'S FINE!

NO. NOT LUBA, SOMEONE ELSE. THINK OF SOMEONE ELSE. LUBA ONLY LEADS TO LAURA.

♪ JESUS ♪

AH, TONANTZIN! THERE YOU GO. SHE AND JESUS HAD QUITE AN AFFAIR GOING A YEAR OR SO BEFORE HE WAS SENT HERE. LOVELY, VIVIFYING, SERENE TONANTZIN...

SUCCESS. LAURA IS NOWHERE TO BE FOUND IN HIS FANTASIES OF TONANTZIN... BUT IT IS TOO LATE: TRYING NOT TO THINK OF SOMETHING USUALLY LEADS TO THINKING ABOUT IT...

7

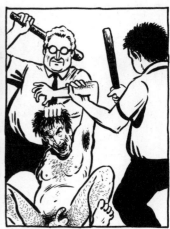

Gilbert Hernandez

The Reticent Hear

The Reticent Heart

Gilbert Hernandez

103

The Reticent Heart

LOOK, I DON'T DESCRIBE THINGS VERY WELL. I'M NO WRITER. I SOMETIMES FORGET WHAT I'M SAYING, UH... IN MID-SENTENCE WHETHER I'M TALKING TO ONE PERSON OR TO ONE THOUSAND. ANYWAY, I'LL TRY TO MAKE THIS AS QUICK AND EASY AS POSSIBLE ON EVERYONE, OK?

ALL RIGHT, FIRST AND LAST THERE IS CARMEN. PERIOD. CARMEN, MY JEWEL IN THE CROWN, MY SALVATION FROM OBLIVION, MY LIGHT IN THE DARKNESS. CARMEN, THE CENTER OF THE UNIVERSE, THE LOVELIEST GROUP OF MOLECULES EVER TO ASSEMBLE, CARMEN THE ETERNAL FLAME...

CARMEN, CARMEN, CARMEN. MY STRENGTH AND MY WEAKNESS. FIRST AND LAST AND EVERYTHING IN BETWEEN... DO I MAKE MYSELF CLEAR?

for the Love of CARMEN

BETO 86

BY GILBERT `THE ЯUSSIAN NIGHTMAЯE` HEЯNANDEKOV-1986

THIRTEEN YEARS AGO, AFTER MY BIG SISTERS GOT MARRIED AND MOVED AWAY LEAVING ME ALONE WITH MY PARENTS, MOM CONVINCED DAD IT WAS TIME WE GOT OUT OF THE CITY WHERE I WAS RAISED AND WE MOVE TO A NICE, QUIET VILLAGE IN THE SOUTH. WELL, THAT VILLAGE WOULD TURN OUT TO BE OL' PALOMAR.

PALOMAR'S QUITE ISOLATED, EVEN FOR A SMALL TOWN. THE CLOSEST TRAIN STATION IS IN FELIX. THERE'S A PUBLIC BUS THAT COMES UP FROM FELIX BUT THAT'S ONLY IF THE DRIVER ISN'T TOO LAZY AND PRETENDS TO FORGET TO STOP HERE.

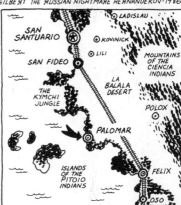

I THOUGHT MY PARENTS WERE JOKING. WE MAY AS WELL HAVE MOVED TO PLUTO! AFTER WE SETTLED IN, I ALMOST CRIED THE FIRST TWO WEEKS WE WERE THERE, I WAS SO MAD AND SCARED AND FRUSTRATED. I WASN'T TO START SCHOOL FOR ANOTHER COUPLE OF MONTHS, SO MOST OF THE TIME I SAT INDOORS LOOKING OUT MY BEDROOM WINDOW IN GROWING FASCINATION THE LOCALS GO ABOUT THEIR PLUVIAN BUSINESS.

WHEN MY FOLKS COULD STAND IT NO LONGER, THEY ORDERED ME TO GO OUT AND MAKE FRIENDS. TO THIS DAY THEY STILL WONDER IF THEY MADE THE RIGHT DECISION, CONSIDERING WHO TURNED OUT TO BE MY FRIENDS...

TRANSLATED BY BIG DADDY HIGGENBOTHAM

Gilbert Hernandez

FIRST THERE WAS VICENTE. DESPITE HIS PROBLEM, HE WAS GENUINELY FRIENDLY AND AGREEABLE; YOU'D FORGET THAT HE SUFFERED FROM ASTHMA TIME TO TIME...

THEN THERE WAS LANKY AND FEY ISRAEL, THE ALWAYS HORNY SATCH, KEYED-UP AND CONFUSED JESUS AND HIS WHACKY LITTLE BROTHER TOCO. AFTER ONLY A WEEK OF HANGING OUT WITH THESE GUYS I COULDN'T IMAGINE LIVING ANYWHERE ELSE.

AS I BEGAN TO APPRECIATE THE BEAUTY OF MY NEW HOME AND ITS GOOD FOLK, THE ANTICS OF ONE PARTICULAR PERSON CAUGHT MY ATTENTION MORE TIMES THAN ANY OTHER.

I GUESS CARMEN JIMENEZ WAS ABOUT ELEVEN, BUT SHE LOOKED EIGHT. I WAS FOUR-TEEN. I DON'T THINK SHE KNEW I WAS EVEN ALIVE THEN.

WHETHER ALONE OR CONSPIRING WITH HER BROTHER AUGUSTIN AND SISTER LUCIA, CARMEN SEEMED **UBIQUITOUS**; ALWAYS POKING IN OTHER PEOPLE'S AFFAIRS, SOMETIMES TO GOOD EFFECT, SOMETIMES NOT. HER POOR OLDER SISTER PIPO WAS ALWAYS THERE AFTERWARDS TO REPAIR THINGS IF CARMEN LEFT THEM TOO BAD.

I REMEMBER TRYING TO TELL MY FRIENDS OF CARMEN'S ESCAPADES, BUT THEY WEREN'T INTERESTED. THEY CONSIDERED CARMEN A CREEP. I DISCOVERED THEN THAT SHE HAD A NOT SO SECRET CRUSH ON ISRAEL. SHE REPULSED HIM, OF COURSE. SOMETIMES I'D WONDER WHY I BOTHERED HANGING OUT WITH THOSE GUYS AT ALL.

I CONTINUED TO ENJOY CARMEN'S ADVENTURES FROM AFAR; I SIMPLY KEPT THINGS TO MYSELF.

IF I COULDN'T ALWAYS TALK TO MY PALS ABOUT PERSONAL THINGS OR WHATEVER, MANUEL ALWAYS HAD TIME TO HEAR ME OUT. MANUEL WAS OLDER BUT HE LIKED ME FOR SOME REASON. I DON'T THINK HE EVER CALLED ME BY MY REAL NAME, THOUGH.

HEY, HERCULES!

The Reticent Hear

MANUEL FELT IT WAS HIS DUTY TO PREPARE ME FOR THE IMMINENT WORLD OF WOMEN AND ROMANCE, BUT HIS POETIC DESCRIPTIONS OF LOVEMAKING WERE TOO ABSTRACT, TOO OBLIQUE FOR THIS ADOLESCENT MIND TO GRASP, SO BEING THE EXPERT MASTURBATOR I WAS, I KEPT IMAGINING A GOOD SNEEZE AT THE END OF A ROLLER COASTER RIDE.

NO ONE COULD HAVE PREPARED ME FOR MY FIRST TIME, ESPECIALLY WHEN YOU CONSIDER IT WAS WITH LA INDIA LUBA...! ONE MINUTE I'M IN HER LIVING ROOM TELLING HER I HAVE TO MY QUIT MY JOB DELIVERING FLYERS FOR HER BATHING BUSINESS, AND THE NEXT MINUTE -- *ZOW!*

YEAH, YEAH, I KNOW WHAT SOME OF YOU GUYS ARE THINKING, BUT I'M TELLING YOU, IT REALLY WASN'T MUCH FUN. MAYBE IF I WAS OLDER, IF I HAD EXPERIENCE, I DON'T KNOW... I MEAN, HELL, I DIDN'T REALLY KNOW WHAT CLOBBERED ME TILL I WAS WELL ON MY WAY HOME.

I REMEMBER SITTING IN MY ROOM SHORTLY AFTER IT HAPPENED AND MY MOTHER WAS TALKING ABOUT A BROKEN LAMP OR SOMETHING. RIGHT THEN I ALMOST TOLD HER, I SWEAR...

I COULDN'T TELL ANYBODY. I DON'T THINK LUBA TOLD ANYBODY EITHER BECAUSE IT'S MY GUESS THAT I WASN'T THE FIRST OR LAST BOY SHE'D PLANNED TO SEDUCE...

THAT SAME NIGHT I DIDN'T SLEEP MUCH. ONE MOMENT I'D FEEL TRIUMPHANT AND THE NEXT DISGUSTED AND HOLLOW...

THE NEXT MORNING I MASTURBATED JUST TO FEEL NORMAL AGAIN, BUT I FELT AWFUL, MAYBE WORSE...

THAT DRY, MATTED HAIR, HER APPALLINGLY OVERSIZED BREASTS, THAT--THAT UNNERVING HUSKY LAUGH... AND THE SMELL, THE SMELL, IT ALL SWAM STRONG IN MY HEAD FOR DAYS AND DAYS...

I THEN DECIDED I HAD TO TELL MY FRIENDS...

ISRAEL WAS IN ONE OF HIS USUAL "HEY LOOK, I'M AN ASS-HOLE" MOODS, SO I WASN'T GOING TO TELL HIM ANYTHING.

I ASKED SATCH WHAT HE'D DO IF LUBA EVER CAME ON TO HIM AND HE ALMOST SHIT. WITH THE FOULEST DESCRIPTIONS OF THE FEMALE BODY I'D EVER HEARD, SATCH MADE IT CLEAR HE WASN'T THE ONE TO TELL.

VICENTE WAS STILL DEPRESSED ABOUT TOCO DYING SUDDENLY THE WEEK BEFORE. I DIDN'T BOTHER TO BRING UP LA INDIA...

FUNNY, BUT JESUS WAS TAKING HIS LITTLE BROTHER'S DEATH REAL WELL, SO I SIMPLY CAME OUT AND ASKED HIM WHAT HE THOUGHT OF LUBA. TURNS OUT HE IS THE LAST GUY I'D EVER TELL OF MY EXPERIENCE!

HE WAS, IS, AND PROBABLY ALWAYS WILL BE CRAZY ABOUT THE WOMAN. AND IT ISN'T JUST AN ADOLESCENT INFATUATION; NO, HIS FEELINGS ARE INDEED GENUINE. TOO BAD MY EX-PERIENCE WITH HER WASN'T HIS. BUT THAT'S FATE, HMM?

Gilbert Hernandez

WHEN I FOUND MANUEL HE WAS TOO BUSY HAVING HIS SECRET LOVE AFFAIR WITH PIPO BEING REVEALED TO THE WORLD BY PIPOLIN HERSELF. I DECIDED THEN I WOULDN'T TELL ANYBODY, PERHAPS NEVER.

HA HA HO HO HAR HAR

@#*¢6..:

THAT WAS THE FIRST TIME I SAW LUBA SINCE THAT NIGHT... AND THE LAST TIME I SAW MANUEL ALIVE.

WHAT WITH TOCO SUCCUMBING TO A COUGH, LUBA SEDUCING ME, THEN MANUEL BEING SHOT TO DEATH BY HIS EX-LOVER SOLEDAD, AND ALL THIS HAPPENING WITHIN WEEKS OF ONE ANOTHER--! WELL. FOR SOME ODD REASON I NOSE DIVED INTO A DEEP DEPRESSION...

I BEGAN TO LOOSEN UP A BIT WHEN I STARTED SECONDARY SCHOOL. I QUICKLY MADE NEW FRIENDS THERE AND BECAME DISTANT TO THE GOINGS ON BACK HOME...

I DIDN'T HANG OUT MUCH ANY MORE...

THEN THERE WERE THE GIRLS IN SCHOOL! THE GIRLS!! I MUST HAVE BEEN THE WORLD'S HORNIEST HUMAN BEING BY THEN. SHORT, TALL, THIN, FAT, PRETTY, NOT SO PRETTY, I WANTED THEM ALL! EVEN THE SHALLOW, MATERIALISTIC GASHEADS! YOW!

I HAD FINALLY GOTTEN A HANDLE ON WHAT MANUEL WAS TALKING ABOUT!

I BEGAN TO THINK ABOUT HAVING REAL CONTACT WITH SOME OF THESE GIRLS AND I BECAME UNSETTLED. WOULD SEX WITH ONE OF THESE BEAUTIES BE LIKE IT WAS WITH LUBA? I GOT NAUSEOUS JUST THINKING ABOUT IT...!

I GOT DEPRESSED. I BEGAN TO HATE WHAT LUBA DID TO ME. I BEGAN TO HATE HER.

BACK IN PALOMAR MY BUDDIES WERE DEALING WITH THEIR SEXUAL URGES THE WAY NORMAL TEENAGE BOYS DO: AND POOR TONANTZIN VILLASEÑOR WAS ONLY TOO HAPPY TO OBLIGE THEM. I HAD NO PART IN IT.

THEN I WENT AWAY TO COLLEGE. THE SCHOOL WAS UP NORTH AND I MAJORED IN MUSIC. IT WAS THE FIRST TIME I LIVED AWAY FROM MY PARENTS. DAD'S WORK SENT THEM BOTH TO LIVE IN COLOMBIA, SO I DIDN'T KNOW WHERE I WAS GOING TO GO AFTER I GRADUATED. AND I KIND OF LIKED THAT FEELING OF... OF FREEDOM, I GUESS...

SECONDARY SCHOOL - HIGH SCHOOL TO US.

IN COLLEGE I ENJOYED THE COMPANY OF FOLKS WHO APPRECIATED DISCUSSING THE LIKES OF EZRA POUND, POLITICS, VAN GOGH, THE IMPORTANCE OF DARK BEER...

MY FEW ENCOUNTERS WITH IGNORANCE WERE WHEN PALOMAR WAS MENTIONED. IT WAS CONSIDERED A JOKE TOWN FILLED WITH RAVISHING CRO-MAGNON WOMEN IDIOTS AND MONGOLOID THUGS. BUT I WAS THE EXCEPTION, OF COURSE. I'M ONE OF THE GOOD ONES, YOU KNOW.

SHALLOW, MATERIALISTIC GASHEADS - YUPPIES

SOMETIMES WHEN I WAS ALONE I'D RECALL THE GOOD TIMES I HAD IN PALOMAR. THEN I'D WORRY ABOUT VICENTE'S FUTURE. I RECOGNIZED I WAS LUCKY TO HAVE WHAT I HAD, BUT WHERE'D THAT LEAVE MY FRIENDS?!

The Reticent Hea

MY COLLEGE MATES WERE WRONG ABOUT PALOMAR, OF COURSE. IT DIDN'T MATTER, ANY WAY... PALOMAR NEVER NEEDED THE REST OF THE WORLD'S PERMISSION TO EXIST.

I WENT THROUGH FOUR YEARS OF COLLEGE WITHOUT ONCE BECOMING INTIMATE WITH A WOMAN.

I GRADUATED AND DECIDED TO RETURN TO PALOMAR. I GOT A JOB TEACHING MUSIC AT A SCHOOL OUTSIDE OF TOWN.

THINGS DIDN'T CHANGE MUCH, WHICH PLEASED ME. THE FABULOUS CHELO WAS STILL GOING STRONG AS SHERIFF, STILL NO PHONES OR TELEVISION, AND STILL NO FEMALE OVER THIRTEEN WOULD EVER BE CAUGHT DEAD WEARING TROUSERS...

AS FOR MY OL' PALS, SATCH WAS MARRIED WITH TWO KIDS AND LIVING IN FELIX, ISRAEL AND VICENTE WERE RAISING HELL IN SAN FIDEO AND JESUS WAS GETTING MARRIED.

I MET LUBA ON THE STREET AND SHE TREATED ME LIKE AN OLD FRIEND, EVEN IF SHE KEPT FORGETTING MY NAME. WE SETTLED ON HERCULES AND IT'S STUCK SINCE.

I WASN'T MAD AT HER ANY MORE. I THINK I HAD EVEN MISSED HER A LITTLE...

IT WAS AT JESUS' WEDDING WHERE I FIRST SAW MY BUDDIES TOGETHER AGAIN. HOME COOKING WAS ALREADY RESHAPING SATCH'S FIGURE, CITY LIFE WAS MAKING ISRAEL CYNICAL, WHILE IT WAS HAVING NO EFFECT ON VICENTE AT ALL. POOR JESUS LOOKED MORE CONFUSED THAN EVER. EVEN THEN I KNEW HIS MARRIAGE WOULDN'T LAST. GOD, HOW I MISSED THOSE GUYS!

TONANTZIN HAD VERY MUCH GROWN UP AND HASN'T LET ANYONE FORGET IT SINCE.

JESUS AND LAURA GOMEZ WERE MARRIED THREE YEARS. SHE WAS A DECENT SORT. SHE AND JESUS SIMPLY DID NOT BELONG ON THE SAME PLANET TOGETHER, THAT'S ALL.

AND THEN...THERE SHE WAS. SHE OFFERED ME A FRIED BABOSA, BUT I DIDN'T RECOGNIZE HER AT FIRST; WHEN I DID, I SHUDDERED AS IF AN ICE-CUBE WAS SHOVED UP MY ASS.

WE STUMBLED AROUND SMALL TALK. SHE SEEMED REALLY IMPRESSED WITH MY, ER, ACADEMIC STANDING, EVEN IF SHE KEPT FORGETTING MY NAME. BUT I WAS USED TO THAT.

ISRAEL INTERRUPTED AND STARTED UP WITH HIS USUAL CRUDE REMARKS ABOUT WOMEN IN GENERAL, AS IF HE WAS SEEING JUST HOW FAR HE COULD GO BEFORE CARMEN FLIPPED.

WELL, SHE DIDN'T. INSTEAD, SHE STOOD THERE AND TOOK EVERY BIT, AS IF SHE DESERVED IT OR SOMETHING ...!

I GUESS I HAD ONE DRINK TOO MANY, BECAUSE THE NEXT THING I KNOW--

THEN I FELT LIKE SHIT. EVERYBODY KNOWS THAT ISRAEL HAS NEVER HIT ANYONE SMALLER THAN HIMSELF, SO HE JUST CUSSED ME OUT AND WALKED AWAY.

IT WAS THE FIRST AND LAST TIME ANYBODY EVER CALLED ME A BULLY. AND IT WAS FROM CARMEN.

Gilbert Hernandez

AS TIME PASSED WE'D SEE EACH OTHER ON THE STREET AND SAY A FEW FRIENDLY WORDS. SHE SEEMED TO GET PRETTIER EVERY TIME I SAW HER. NO, MAKE THAT GODDAMN BEAUTIFUL.

THEY SAY IF YOU'RE NERVOUS BEING AROUND SOMEONE, SIMPLY PICTURE THEM NAKED AND YOU'LL COME TO RELAX...

HELL, I PICTURED CARMEN NAKED ALL THE TIME, AND IT MADE ME FEEL ANYTHING BUT RELAXED...!

IT WAS WHEN I ACCIDENTLY DROPPED MY BRIEFCASE AND WE BOTH REACHED FOR IT THAT I KNEW..!

MY BODY SURGED WITH AN ENERGY I THOUGHT WAS ONLY RESERVED FOR BODYBUILDERS OR HONEST EVANGELISTS! CARMEN MUST HAVE EXPERIENCED A SIMILAR JOLT, BECAUSE SHE LOOKED AT ME THE WAY A CAT DOES WHEN YOU SURPRISE IT AND TOOK OFF LIKE A FLASH.

THAT WAS ALL I NEEDED TO KNOW. THE VERY NEXT DAY I WENT UP TO SAN FIDEO TO SEE PIPO...

EVEN THOUGH IT WAS OBVIOUS HER HUSBAND GATO WAS DOING VERY WELL FOR HIS FAMILY, THINGS MUST HAVE BEEN DULL FOR PIPO. SHE WAS REALLY HAPPY TO SEE ME. AND WE HAD NEVER EVEN BEEN INTRODUCED BEFORE THEN.

MAN, THAT WOMAN CAN TALK. SHE ACTED LIKE LUBA DID WHEN I FIRST CAME BACK, TREATING ME LIKE AN OLD FRIEND, REMINISCING THE GOOD OL' DAYS. I COULD SENSE SHE STILL HADN'T GOTTEN OVER MANUEL.

WHEN HER MONOLOGUE FINALLY SWUNG MY WAY, I BLURTED OUT THE FACT THAT I WANTED TO MARRY HER SISTER. PIPO'S EYES LIT UP.

PIPO FELT HER SISTER LUCIA WOULD MAKE A GOOD WIFE, BUT DIDN'T I THINK SHE WAS A LITTLE YOUNG STILL?

I TOLD HER I WANTED TO MARRY CARMEN, NOT LUCIA.

YOU SHOULD HAVE SEEN PIPO'S FACE.

SHE SAT QUIET FOR A MOMENT AS IF I HAD TOLD HER MANUEL WAS ACTUALLY STILL ALIVE.

SHE SMILED AND WISHED ME LUCK.

WHEN I LEFT I COULD SWEAR I HEARD PIPO BEHIND THE DOOR LAUGHING...

A MORNING OR SO LATER I FIGURED I WAS A NUT. I DIDN'T EVEN KNOW CARMEN. NOT REALLY. FOOL.

I DIDN'T GO TO WORK THAT DAY. I PUT ON MY BEST SUNDAY SUIT AND AT A GOOD DISTANCE I CIRCLED CARMEN'S HOUSE ALL DAY LONG TILL IT WAS DARK.

I COULDN'T BRING MYSELF TO KNOCK ON THE DOOR OR TO GO AWAY. I NEVER SAW ANYONE ENTER OR LEAVE THE HOUSE IN ALL THAT TIME.

MAYBE I WAS HOPING SOMEBODY INSIDE MIGHT NOTICE ME AND CALL ME OVER. MAYBE I WAS A BLASTED IDIOT.

I FELT LIKE A FOOL FOR MISSING WORK AND SHOWED UP AS USUAL THE NEXT DAY.

BUT WHEN I GOT HOME I SNUCK UP ON SOMEBODY'S ROOF AND SAT THERE WATCHING CARMEN'S HOUSE BLOCKS AWAY.

I SAW CARMEN AND HER FAMILY IN AND OUT ALL AFTERNOON. I STAYED UP THERE UNTIL NIGHT AND WHEN FINALLY THE LAST LIGHT WAS OUT, I WENT HOME. WITH A COLD.

The Reticent Heart

THE NEXT DAY I DITCHED WORK AGAIN. I AGAIN PUT ON MY BEST SUIT AND AGAIN I CIRCLED CARMEN'S HOUSE AT THAT COMFORTABLE DISTANCE.

THIS TIME I SAW AUGUSTIN AND LUCIA IN AND OUT ALL DAY, BUT NO CARMEN.

FEELING VERY STUPID AND USE-LESS, I STARTED HOME. THEN I HEARD LOUD LAUGHING FROM THE HOUSE. I SWEAR, IT SOUNDED LIKE PIPO AND CARMEN! I TRIED TO GET AWAY AS FAST AS I COULD WITHOUT BLOWING IT.

I DIDN'T GO HOME. I WENT TO THE BAR AND GOT SMASHED.

NEXT THING I KNOW I'M BANGING MY HEAD AGAINST THE RAILROAD TRACKS WHICH LIE OVER TEN KILOMETERS FROM TOWN...

I HAD A LOT OF TIME TO THINK ABOUT WHAT I WAS DOING AS I WALKED HOME.

I MANAGED TO MAKE IT INTO TOWN BEFORE NOON WITHOUT BEING SEEN BY ANYONE I KNEW.

AT HOME I GOT CLEANED UP AND CHANGED MY SUIT. I SAT INSIDE ALL DAY AND WAITED FOR THE NIGHT. THEN I WENT OUT.

UPON REACHING THE ISLAND, I HEADED STRAIGHT FOR THE MAIN VILLAGE.

I GAVE THEM TWO HUNDRED AND EIGHTEEN FRANCS, SIX BACK ISSUES OF COSMOPOLITAN, AND A FRAMED AUTOGRAPHED PHOTO OF AMERICAN FILM STAR CONRAD BAIN. IN RETURN I WAS GIVEN THE WORKS.

I KNOCKED THREE TIMES AND LUCIA OPENED UP AND LET ME IN...

I ASKED CARMEN'S MOTHER ELVIRA FOR CARMEN'S HAND IN MARRIAGE. ELVIRA LOOKED AT ME LIKE I WAS MAKING FUN OF HER.

IN ELVIRA'S OWN WORDS: " IT WAS JUST ME AND MY LITTLE PIPO IN THOSE DAYS. BEFORE THE TOURISTS DISCOVERED THE SWAP MEET, WHEN YOU COULD STILL HAGGLE OR TRADE, BEFORE THE FIXED PRICES AND GOVERNMENT TAXES..."

"AND THERE BETWEEN THE BLIVITZ VENDOR AND THE WORLD'S WORST POTTERY SAT THE DEMON ALL ALONE. PINNED TO HER SACK WAS THE NOTE WHICH READ 'GOOD RIDDANCE.' I STILL HAVE THAT NOTE SOMEWHERE ..."

NATURALLY I WAS DISGUSTED THAT THE SWAP MEET HAD SUNK THIS LOW. I CURSED THEM ALL AND THEIR GRANDMOTHERS AS WELL. THEN I BROUGHT THE CHILD HOME WITH ME."

SHE WAS THE MOST WELL-BEHAVED CHILD I HAD EVER SEEN. PIPO WAS JEALOUS AND TEASED HER A LOT, BUT THE CHILD NEVER WHINED ONCE. I NAMED HER CARMEN AFTER MY GREAT GRANDMOTHER WHO FOUGHT IN THE LEGENDARY SIX DAY LAUNDRY WAR ...

WHEN SHE FINALLY DECIDED TO SPEAK, THE THINGS THAT CAME OUT OF THAT TINY MOUTH COULD HAVE TURNED THE NASTIEST OF CONVICTS WHITE...!"

"WHEN SHE GOT OLDER IT WAS WORSE. SHE WOULD INSULT PEOPLE, ANYBODY WITH THE COLDEST, CRUELEST WORDS... AND SO QUIETLY, SO SERIOUS... NO MATTER HOW BAD I PUNISHED HER SHE WOULDN'T STOP. SHE DOES IT TO THIS DAY. PEOPLE DON'T TALK TO HER MUCH BECAUSE WHO KNOWS IF SHE'LL BE IN ONE OF HER MOODS? I'VE KNOWN THOSE WHO'VE WANTED TO KILL HER...!'

THEN WHEN ELVIRA WAS THROUGH SHE ASKED ME IF I STILL WANTED CARMEN. I SAID YES. ELVIRA THOUGHT FOR A MINUTE AND THEN SIGHED, WHISPERING SOMETHING TO HERSELF THAT MAY HAVE BEEN GOOD RIDDANCE.

IT FELT LIKE I WAS LEFT ALONE IN THE ROOM LONG ENOUGH TO FINISH HALF OF WAR AND PEACE. WHEN CARMEN FINALLY ENTERED SHE DIDN'T LOOK OLDER THAN TWELVE...

I LET HER HAVE IT, BOTH BARRELS. I COULDN'T STOP MYSELF. I TALKED AND TALKED AND TALKED HOPING TO CONVINCE HER I WASN'T JUST SOME LOCO OFF THE STREET. OF COURSE, I PROBABLY SOUNDED JUST LIKE SOME LOCO OFF THE STREET...

The Reticent Heart

THEN WHEN I FINALLY PAUSED TO CATCH MY BREATH, SHE SPOKE. SHE ASKED ME IF I HAD EVER HAD SEX WITH ANYONE BEFORE. FLAT OUT, JUST LIKE THAT, COMPLETELY SERIOUS...

MY MIND ANSWERED "YES," BUT MY MOUTH SAID "NO." I DON'T KNOW WHY I SAID NO BUT IT WAS WHAT SHE WANTED TO HEAR BECAUSE THEN SHE AGREED TO MARRY ME. FLAT OUT, JUST LIKE THAT...

WE SET THE DATE AND EVERYTHING WAS GOING GREAT! I FELT STRONG AND CONFIDENT AND MY PARENTS WERE HAPPY AND MY BUDDIES THOUGHT I WAS LOCO BUT WERE HAPPY FOR ME JUST THE SAME AND THE FOLKS IN TOWN WERE HAPPY --

THEN..!

...I BEGAN HAVING SERIOUS DOUBTS. I STARTED GETTING NERVOUS AND CONFUSED.

DOUBT TURNED TO PARANOIA WHICH TURNED TO NEAR PANIC..!

CARMEN ONLY AGREED TO MARRY ME BECAUSE SHE THOUGHT I WAS A VIRGIN; AT LEAST THAT'S WHAT I CONVINCED MYSELF.

I WAS OBSESSED WITH THIS PREDICAMENT! IN MY FEVERED MIND MY LITTLE LIE TOOK ON GALACTIC PROPORTIONS!

I FIGURED IT WAS THE WORK I GOT ON THE ISLAND! WERE THE EFFECTS WEARING OFF, OR DID THE INDIANS RECOGNIZE THE QUESTIONABLE VALUE OF MY TRADE AND BEGIN TO SOMEHOW REVERSE THE PROCESS? I RESIGNED MYSELF TO THE LATTER EXPLANATION, OF COURSE. GOD, WAS I A WRECK!

I WENT TO THE BAR TO TRY TO DRINK MYSELF INTO SOME KIND OF ANSWER. AFTER KNOCKING BACK A FEW I HEADED STRAIGHT FOR LUBA'S HOUSE.

I BURST IN WITHOUT KNOCKING, LIKE SOMEONE READY TO ANNOUNCE TO HIS FAMILY THAT WORLD WAR THREE HAD FINALLY BEGUN ...!

I TOLD LUBA THAT CARMEN MUST NEVER FIND OUT ABOUT THAT NIGHT. I MUST HAVE LOOKED PRETTY BAD, PRETTY SERIOUS, BECAUSE LUBA IMMEDIATELY AGREED. I'M NOT SURE NOW THAT SHE REALLY KNEW WHAT I WAS TALKING ABOUT...

I APOLOGIZED FOR BEING A JERK AND AS I BEGAN TO LEAVE I FELT MY CONFIDENCE RAPIDLY RETURNING! I BEGAN TO FEEL STRONG, LIKE THE TIME CARMEN AND I FIRST TOUCHED HANDS--!

FROM BEHIND ME I COULD HEAR LUBA IN A MOCKING VOICE, "GOOD LUCK ON YOUR IMPRISONMENT--OH, I MEAN MARRIAGE, GUY..."

I DIDN'T CARE. I COULD HAVE KICKED LARRY HOLMES' ASS THE WAY I WAS FEELING...!

OUR WEDDING WAS NICE; NO FIGHTS, NO BARFING...

THAT NIGHT AS WE PREPARED FOR BED, I BEGAN TO FEEL A LITTLE GUILTY FOR WANTING HER SO BAD, LIKE SOME DROOLING, SLOBBERING JOHN...

I GOT OVER THAT QUICK ENOUGH, THOUGH.

ALL I WILL SAY ABOUT OUR FIRST NIGHT TOGETHER IS THAT IT WAS FAR LOVLIER THAN WHAT'S DELINEATED IN THOSE BOGUS LETTERS TO PENTHOUSE MAGAZINE MONTH AFTER MONTH...

9

WE'VE BEEN MARRIED FOR FOUR YEARS NOW. CARMEN GETS PRETTY SCARED NOW AND THEN BECAUSE SHE DOESN'T KNOW WHO SHE REALLY IS OR WHERE SHE'S FROM...

CARMEN HANGS OUT WITH TONANTZIN A LOT. GOD, AND WHEN THOSE TWO ARE TOGETHER NO ONE IS SAFE. I LOVE MY WIFE, BUT MAN, CAN SHE BE A JERK...!

TONANTZIN'S QUITE THE HOMEWRECKER, YOU KNOW. DRESSES UP LIKE SOME CARTOON WHORE AND MANIPULATES THE WEAKER GUYS' LIVES JUST FOR THE FUN OF IT. AND CARMEN CONDONES IT! WELL, MAYBE IT IS FAIR. ONCE THE EXPLOITED, NOW THE EXPLOITER. PERSONALLY, I THINK THE GIRL'S A BIT OF A CREEP.

CARMEN KNOWS NOW ABOUT THAT NIGHT WITH ME AND LUBA. EVEN THOUGH IT HAPPENED LONG BEFORE WE WERE MARRIED, CARMEN WAS SURE TO BRING IT UP WHENEVER SHE WAS LOSING AN ARGUMENT, SAYING I WAS A LIAR AND THAT I TRICKED HER INTO MARRIAGE, BLAH-BLAH...

WELL... SHE DOESN'T BRING IT UP IN FIGHTS ANY MORE; NOT AFTER HER LITTLE 'THING' WITH ISRAEL.

THREE MONTHS AGO, RIGHT AFTER DINNER, OUT OF THE BLUE CARMEN BROKE DOWN CRYING AND CONFESSED TO CHEATING ON ME.

ABOUT A YEAR AGO WHILE I WAS AT WORK ISRAEL WAS IN TOWN VISITING HIS FOLKS. CARMEN SAW HIM AND INVITED HIM IN. THEY TALKED ABOUT OLD TIMES AND CRAP LIKE THAT AND... WELL, SHE CLAIMS NOBODY PLANNED IT, IT JUST HAPPENED. I CAN FUCKING IMAGINE...

SHE TELLS ME WHEN IT WAS OVER BOTH SHE AND ISRAEL FELT SO ROTTEN THAT HE PROMISED HER HE'D NEVER RETURN TO PALOMAR AGAIN.

AS IT TURNS OUT, CARMEN GOT PREGNANT. CONVINCED IT WAS ISRAEL'S KID AND NOT MINE, CARMEN HAD IT ABORTED. SHE DID IT FOR FEAR THAT I'D FIND OUT WHO'S KID IT WAS SOONER OR LATER AND SHE'D LOSE ME FOR SURE...

IT'S A RARE OCCURRENCE IN OUR PART OF THE COUNTRY WHEN A WOMAN HAS AN ABORTION. IT'S CONSIDERED A MORAL CRIME COMPARABLE TO KILLING ONE'S OWN PARENTS! OR ONE'S OWN CHILDREN.

I TRIED TO COMFORT HER DESPITE MY IMMEDIATE FEELINGS, BUT THAT MADE HER FEEL MORE GUILTY...

SO THERE I WAS, A WALKING TUMOR OF SEETHING FRUSTRATION WITH NO OBVIOUS OUTLET IN SIGHT.

I MEAN, I COULDN'T SOMEHOW PUNISH HER. SHE'D ALREADY SUFFERED ENOUGH, SHE IS SUFFERING TO THIS DAY...

A FEW NIGHTS AFTER SHE GAVE ME THE GOOD NEWS I SNUCK OUT WHILE SHE SLEPT AND I GOT ALARMINGLY DRUNK. I AGAIN FOUND MYSELF BANGING MY HEAD AGAINST THOSE GOOD OL' RAILROAD TRACKS SO FAR FROM HOME...

THIS TIME I MANAGED TO MAKE IT HOME BEFORE DAWN. AND THIS TIME I DIDN'T GO TO THE ISLAND FOR THE WORKS. THIS TIME I CAME HOME TO MY WIFE AND TO MY LIFE...

The Reticent Hea

THE LAST TIME I SAW ISRAEL WAS RIGHT BEFORE HIS AND CARMEN'S THING.

THE AMERICAN PHOTOGRAPHER HOWARD MILLER WAS IN PALOMAR USING OUR TOWN AS THE SUBJECT FOR A PHOTO JOURNAL...

MILLER RELATED TO ME SEVERAL FIRST HAND ACCOUNTS OF WHAT HE'D SEEN IN CAMBODIA, NICARAGUA, SOUTH AFRICA...HE SHOWED ME A FEW SHOTS HE TOOK IN EL SALVADOR I WON'T SOON FORGET. I ASKED HIM WHY PALOMAR, THEN? WE AREN'T NEWS TO ANYBODY. HE *SAID THIS TIME* HE JUST WANTED TO SHOW THE *PURE BEAUTY OF INNOCENCE* INSTEAD OF THE HORROR THAT USUALLY DESTROYS IT.

IT WAS WHEN MILLER BECAME INVOLVED WITH TONANTZIN THAT THINGS WENT TO SHIT.

I DON'T REALLY KNOW WHAT HAPPENED BETWEEN THEM, BUT IT RESULTED IN HIS LEAVING FOR THE STATES IN A HURRY AND TONANTZIN LEFT HURT AND PREGNANT.

CARMEN FLIPPED! HER RACIST TENDENCIES EXPLODED LIKE I'D NEVER SEEN BEFORE! SHE JUST ABOUT BLAMED THE ENTIRE WHITE RACE FOR HURTING TONANTZIN...

SHE WAS OUT OF LINE, SO I LET HER HAVE IT. SO ALL OF A SUDDEN SHE'S A MIND *READER* AND SHE KNEW EXACTLY HOW MILLER FELT ABOUT IT. OF COURSE, CARMEN WENT AFTER ME NEXT...

EVEN AFTER HE WAS LONG GONE I NOTICED A LOT OF FOLKS IN TOWN WERE PRETTY MAD AT MILLER, BUT I COULD SEE THAT MOST OF THEM WERE JUST USING HIM AS AN EXCUSE TO VENT THEIR RACIST ANTI-WHITE AMERICAN BILE IN PUBLIC.

AND EVERYTIME I STUCK UP FOR MILLER, I GOT IT, TOO.

WELL, ALMOST EVERYTIME. I REMEMBER LUBA *BITCHING* ABOUT HOW MILLER WAS CLEARLY EXPLOITING US ALL, AND WAS GOING TO GET RICH AND FAMOUS TO BOOT...!

THIS TIME I CHICKENED OUT AND KEPT MY MOUTH SHUT. I JUST DIDN'T FEEL LIKE HAVING LUBA'S WRATH UPSIDE MY HEAD, TOO...

THEN ISRAEL SPOKE UP AND DEFENDED HIM! ISRAEL SAID MAYBE MILLER WASN'T SUCH A GREAT GUY, BUT IF IT WASN'T FOR HIS BOOK ABOUT PALOMAR, NOBODY MIGHT EVER KNOW WE EVEN EXISTED!

SO WHEN MILLER'S GONE AND WE'RE ALL GONE AND THIS TOWN'S GOOD AND GONE, EITHER FLATTENED BY BOMBS OR HAVING BEEN RENDERED UNRECOGNIZABLE WITH SKYSCRAPERS AND MALLS, HIS BOOK MIGHT BE ALL WHAT'S LEFT OF US...OUR WORLD, OUR LIVES...

IT WAS PROBABLY THE FIRST TIME ISRAEL AND I EVER AGREED ON SOMETHING, EVEN IF IT WAS ONLY PARTIALLY. WHAT *WAS* THE WORLD COMING TO..?

NOW I FIND OUT ABOUT HIM AND MY WIFE, AND -- WELL, THAT'S ALL IN THE PAST, LIFE GOES ON, RIGHT? *SHIT...*

I GOT A LETTER FROM MILLER A FEW WEEKS BACK. HE STILL HASN'T FOUND A PUBLISHER FOR HIS BOOK YET. SAYS HE STILL THINKS OF TONANTZIN A LOT...

Gilbert Hernandez

FUNNY, BUT LUBA AND I HAVE BECOME PRETTY GOOD BUDDIES IN THE LAST YEAR OR SO. CARMEN STILL DOESN'T LIKE HER BUT SHE USUALLY KEEPS QUIET ABOUT IT...

LAST I HEARD OF VICENTE, HE WAS ON HIS WAY TO THE UNITED STATES WITH SOME GUYS TO FIND DECENT WORK. I GET THIS...FEELING, I DON'T KNOW, THIS FEELING THAT I'LL NEVER SEE VICENTE AGAIN. I TRY NOT TO THINK ABOUT IT...

WHAT CAN I SAY ABOUT OL' SATCH. SATCH IS SATCH IS SATCH IS SATCH. ALWAYS AND FOREVER. AT THE RATE HIS WIFE MARTA'S HAVING KIDS, THEY OUGHT TO BE STARTING THEIR OWN COUNTRY SOON.

ISRAEL. HUH. WELL, AS FAR AS I CAN TELL, HE'S KEPT HIS PROMISE TO CARMEN, BECAUSE NOBODY'S SEEN HIM FOR A LONG TIME, NOT EVEN HIS FOLKS. TO BE HONEST, I CAN'T SAY I MISS HIM.

JESUS OUGHT TO BE GETTING OUT OF PRISON SOON IF HE'D ONLY STOP BEATING UP ON THEM GUARDS...

PIPO'S BACK LIVING IN PALOMAR AND IS IN THE PROCESS OF DIVORCING OL' GATO. THIS MAKES CARMEN PRETTY HAPPY, NOT TO MENTION THE LOCAL BACHELORS.

WELL, I GUESS THAT'S ALL...UM, CARMEN'S PREGNANT NOW, SO WE'RE PRETTY HAPPY. I'M A LITTLE WORRIED FOR HER BECAUSE SHE'S SO TINY AND HAVING A KID CAN BE AN ORDEAL. BUT LIFE'S AN ORDEAL SOMETIMES, RIGHT? LIFE, LOVE, IT'S HARD WORK, RIGHT? YEAH, ⸰SIGH.⸰ I'LL ADMIT IT, THOUGH, SOMETIMES WHEN I'M DOWN, SOMETIMES IT ALL JUST MAKES ME WANT TO BANG MY HEAD ON--NAW, NAW, HEH, JUST KIDDING, REALLY... HEH, HEH, JEEZ...

116

The Reticent Hea

THE STIGMATIC:
ONE WHO SOMETIMES
BEARS OPEN SORES CORRESPONDING
IDENTICALLY TO THE WOUNDS
SUFFERED ON THE *CRUCIFIED*
BODY OF JESUS CHRIST..

Gilbert Hernandez

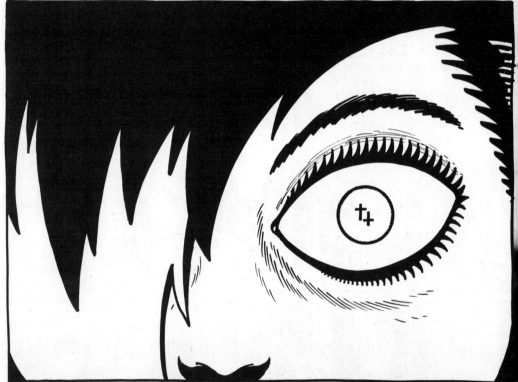

Tears from Heaven

THE LIFE AND TIMES OF ERRATA STIGMATA

BY GILBERT HERNANDEZ ADDITIONAL MATERIAL BY MARIO FEB 85

IT WAS LITTLE ERRATA'S WEALTHY UNCLE IRA AND AUNT ZEPHIE WHO TOOK HER IN AFTER THE TRAGEDY...

WELCOME TO YOUR NEW HOME, ERRATA.

AS TIME PASSED, UNCLE IRA DID HIS BEST TO SHOW US ALL JUST HOW MUCH HE GREW TO ADORE HIS LITTLE POOCHKA...

WHEN IT WAS TIME FOR UNCLE IRA TO DEPART ON A BUSINESS TRIP, ERRATA WAS ALWAYS MORE THAN SAD..

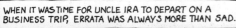

BECAUSE IT WAS AUNT ZEPHIE'S TURN TO PLAY.

4

YOU MUST SIT STILL AND WATCH AUNTIE, ERRATA.

IT IS IMPORTANT THAT YOU LEARN ABOUT HOW LIFE BEGINS, CHILD, SO THAT YOU WILL NEVER BE CONFUSED.

AHHHH...UH...AH-AH..OW! OW! OOHHH...SEE, ERRATA? UGH... MM--MM ...OHHH...UGNH...OW..OW! OH! OH! OW!

LATER THAT NIGHT, AS SHE SLEPT, ERRATA DID NOT DREAM...

The Reticent Hea

Gilbert Hernandez

AND WHEN AUNTIE ZEPHIE WASN'T SHOWING ERRATA WHAT LIFE WAS ABOUT, THE CHILD LEARNED FROM OTHER SOURCES...

ERRATA, DEAR. TIME FOR YOUR PIANO LESSONS.

PLINK PLINK PLONK

NO, NO, CHILD. TRY IT AGAIN.

PLINK PLINK PLONK

NO·NO·NO!

THE NOTE IS A!

A!

A!

WHOK

TEACHER GETS VERY IMPATIENT WITH TALENTLESS SWINE WHO BUTCHER THAT WHAT IS MEANT TO BE HEARD IN HEAVEN...

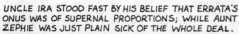

The Reticent Heart

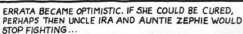

ERRATA BECAME OPTIMISTIC. IF SHE COULD BE CURED, PERHAPS THEN UNCLE IRA AND AUNTIE ZEPHIE WOULD STOP FIGHTING...

STRIP 'ER DOWN TO HER CHONERS. THIS WON'T TAKE TOO LONG.

BE STILL, CHILD.

I'M GONNA BE CURED.. I'M GONNA BE CURED.. I'M GONNA BE CURED..

WHAT'S THAT STINK, AUNTIE?

IT'S CALLED SULFUR, CHILD. IT'S YOUR VERY OWN SPECIAL MEDICINE.

ENTER, LADIES.

DON'T BE SHY, ERRATA. IT WON'T HURT A BIT.

FOUR THOUSAND KILOMETERS AWAY, AT THE VERY SAME MOMENT OF ERRATA'S FIRST TREATMENT, UNCLE IRA SUFFERED A MYSTERIOUS SEIZURE ...

UUUUGGGGHHAAAHH...

ERRATA, SWEETHEART? ARE YOU AWAKE?

YES, UNCA IRA.

COME ON. YOU AND I ARE GOING AWAY, DEAR. WOULD YOU LIKE THAT?

NO MORE DEAD? NO MORE CURE? NO MORE..?

10

IT WAS WHEN *PASSING THROUGH PALO POLA* WHERE ERRATA REVEALED THE EFFECTIVENESS OF HER TREATMENTS TO BE A LOAD OF, SHALL WE SAY, BOVINE EXCREMENT.

IT TOOK THAT ALMOST FATAL SEIZURE TO OPEN IRA'S EYES TO WHAT WAS HAPPENING AT HOME WHEN HE WAS AWAY...

...THE BLEEDING BEGINS AFTER SHE'S WITNESSED OR EXPERIENCED SOMETHING FRIGHTENING TO HER MIND. SOMETHING OF TERRIBLE INJUSTICE OR OF IN-HUMAN CRUELTY. OR EVEN SOMETIMES IF SHE'S SIMPLY SEEN A CAR RUN OVER A DOGGIE...

YES, WELL, MY AMBROSE YAK YAK BLAH BLAH...

YAK YAK YAK

CONVENTION →

ERRATA HAD NEVER BEEN HAPPIER. TO MEET SOMEONE LIKE OONA WAS BEYOND HER WILDEST DREAMS...

I WISH WE COULD BE SISTERS AND PLAY WITH EACH OTHER FOREVER AND EVER...

ME TOO. I GOT A LOT OF BROTHERS AND SIS-TERS BUT NOBODY LIKE ME.

MY MOMMY SAYS I'M SPECIAL 'CAUSE GOD PICKED ME.

← CONVENTIO

ME TOO, THEN! I'M SPECIAL TOO 'CAUSE GOD PICKED ME, TOO!

EXCEPT MY AUNTIE GETS MAD WHEN I GET MY DRESS ALL DIRTY WITH BLOOD.

WANNA HEAR A BIG FAT SECRET? I KNOW ABOUT ANOTHER PLACE ON US WHERE ME AND YOU WILL HAVE BLOOD WHEN WE'RE BIGGER...

Now Errata was pleased. As long as Auntie Zephie bled too, Errata would be gratified...

The Reticent Hear

A TRUE STORY

BY BETO JAN-FEB 86

THIS WAS ABOUT TEN YEARS AGO. A FRIEND OF MINE AND I ARE SITTING AROUND AT A TEACHER FRIEND'S HOUSE WATCHING T.V. WHEN WRESTLING COMES ON.

I HADN'T WATCHED WRESTLING SINCE I WAS A KID. THIS ONE GUY COMES ON AND HE'S FLIPPING ABOUT PUTTING ON A SHOW WORTHY OF THE VETERAN GRAPPLERS OF MY YOUTH.

I'M REMINDED OF GREATS LIKE BOBO BRAZIL, MAGNIFICENT MAURICE, THE DESTROYER AND THE FABULOUS MOOLAH! MOOLAH JUST SO HAPPENS TO BE AT THIS MOMENT THE WOMEN'S CHAMPION. SHE ORIGINALLY WON THE TITLE IN 1956! WOTTA GAL!

MONTHS LATER, WRESTLING COMES TO MY TOWN EVERY THURSDAY NIGHT. MY YOUNGER BROTHER ATTENDS AND LATER TELLS ME OF THIS ONE GUY HE SAW WHO FIT THE DESCRIPTION OF THE GUY I SAW ON T.V.. TURNS OUT HIS NAME IS GORGEOUS KEITH FRANKS.

I MYSELF BRAVE THE LOCAL MATCHES AND WITNESS THE MAN AT WORK MYSELF. I AM NOT DISAPPOINTED.

LATER, POP SINGER DEBBIE HARRY IS FEATURED ON THE COVER OF A WRESTLING MAGAZINE. I ALWAYS DID THINK ROCK 'N' ROLL AND WRESTLING WERE A LOT ALIKE. ANYWAY, THE LOCAL GIGS COME TO A CLOSE AND AS LIFE GOES ON GRAPPLING AND GORGEOUS KEITH FRANKS FADE FROM OUR LOCAL T.V. STATION, AND MY MIND AS WELL.

Gilbert Hernandez

133

SEVERAL YEARS PASS AND ONE DAY I NOTICE MY YOUNGER BROTHER WATCHING WRESTLING ON T.V.. I HADN'T KNOWN IT WAS BACK ON THE AIR LOCALLY AND AM AMUSED THAT SINGER CYNDI LAUPER'S BEING INTERVIEWED BY ROWDY RODDY PIPER.

LAUPER'S INVOLVEMENT IN WRESTLING BRINGS SO MUCH MEDIA ATTENTION THAT THE 'SPORT' ENJOYS A COMEBACK LIKE IT HASN'T SEEN SINCE ITS HEY-DAY IN THE 50'S!

··PERSONALLY, I THINK THE NUMBER ONE FRENCH-MAN RENÉ GOULET A.K.A. THE MICHAEL JACKSON OF WRESTLING HAS A GOOD SHOT AT THE TITLE.

HE COULD NEVER BEAT FIT FINLEY, THOUGH.

PTCH..! IT'S THE WORST, THE WORST. IN MY DAY... HARUMF..

ABDULLAH THE BUTCHER

BOLO

JOE LeDUC

KEVIN SULLIVAN

THE AMERICAN DREAM DUSTY RHODES

ADRIAN ADONIS

BOOGIE WOOGIE MAN JIMMY VALIANT

KING KONG BUNDY

LITTLE BEAVER

THAT'S RIGHT! GORGEOUS KEITH FRANKS IS BACK WITH A BRAND NEW IDENTITY! MY GIRLFRIEND AND SOME FRIENDS ATTEND A WRESTLING GIG IN L.A. WHERE ADRIAN ADONIS APPEARS, BUT HE IS NOT WELL RECEIVED BY THE AUDIENCE.

BOO FATSO LARDBUTT HAR BOO BOO

AAH-SHADDAP !!!!!!

THEN, THE FATEFUL NIGHT: MY GIRLFRIEND AND I SHOW UP AT A GIG WHERE ADONIS IS TO APPEAR. MY GIRLFRIEND IS A PHOTOGRAPHER AND WANTS TO GET SHOTS OF SOME OF THE GRAPPLERS AS THEY ENTER THE BUILDING.

DO YOU THINK ADONIS WILL GET MAD IF I TAKE HIS PICTURE WHEN HE COMES IN?

NAW! I'M SURE HE'LL BE COOL! GO AHEAD!

2

The Reticent Heart

LOOK! THERE HE IS IN THE PHONE BOOTH.

HE'S STICKING HIS TONGUE OUT AT US. WHAT A CARD! WE'LL GET THE SHOT WHEN HE'S DONE.

WE WAIT FOR ABOUT 10 MINUTES, WHEN FINALLY...

OH, I'M SCARED. MAYBE I SHOULDN'T...

AW, GO AHEAD!

HEY... HE LOOKS KINDA MAD OR SOMETHING.

H-HI. CAN I TAKE YOUR PICTURE?

@#*@ MUMBLE MUMBLE... FREE ENTERPRISE, RIGHT..? ¡#*@⨍FUKN..@#*⁊s ...BULL SHIT...

HEY... HEY, HE YOUR BOYFRIEND? HEY...!

IS HE YOUR BOYFRIEND?!

YEAH...

FUCKN... @#⨅⨅⨅.... ...AND PEE WEE HERMAN... @#*⨅ and all ⨅...

WE DECIDE TO SIT DOWN AND REFLECT UPON WHAT THE HELL HAD JUST HAPPENED. A POPCORN VENDOR WALKS UP TO TALK TO A NEARBY SECURITY GUARD...

← EXIT →

DID YOU HEAR THAT?

COULDN'T UNDERSTAND A GODDAMN WORD HE SAID...

HE SAID ONE OF THE WRESTLERS ORDERED A BUNCH OF FOOD FROM THE CONCESSION STAND AND TOOK IT WITHOUT PAYING! THEN HE THREATENED THE LADIES BEHIND THE COUNTER TILL THEY HAD TO CALL SECURITY! I'LL BET IT WAS ADONIS!

3

Gilbert Hernandez

WE THEN HEAR STORIES ABOUT A WRESTLER WHO'D BEEN PICKING FIGHTS AND STUFF WITH FANS ALL NIGHT..!

DID YOU HEAR WHAT HE SAID ABOUT MY MOTHER? I DIDN'T EVEN KNOW WHAT HE SAID SHE KNEW HIM!

THE MATCHES GET UNDERWAY AND WE'RE SURE ADONIS WON'T WRESTLE, NOT IN HIS 'CONDITION.' THE FIRST MATCH IS WITH S.D. JONES AND IRON MIKE SHARPE. IN THE HEAT OF BATTLE SHARPE EXITS THE RING TO ESCAPE TO THE LOCKER ROOM, BUT INSTEAD HEADS OUR WAY --

GRRAURR...

AW, SHIT, HERE WE GO AGAIN...

BUT TO MY SURPRISE, SHARPE IS A REAL GENTLEMAN! AS HE'S ABOUT TO WIPE HIS SOPPING BROW HE NOTICES ME IN THE AISLE SEAT AND STOPS HIMSELF IN MID-MOTION AS NOT TO DRIP SWEAT IN MY BEER. MY FAITH IN HUMANITY IS RESTORED...FOR THE MOMENT.

THEN, AFTER A COUPLE OF MORE MATCHES...

--ADRIAN ADONIS!

BOO BOO BOO BOO

I DON'T BELIEVE IT!? THEY'RE GONNA LET HIM..?!

THE MAN IS OBVIOUSLY OUT OF IT. HE'S STAGGERING AND STRUTTING ALL OVER THE RING MAKING LEWD GESTURES TO THE AUDIENCE. AT WOMEN AND KIDS, TOO! THEN, ALL WITHIN TWO MINUTES, WITHOUT EVEN REMOVING HIS JACKET:

HE DEMOLISHES HIS OPPONENT IN SECONDS FLAT (AND IT LOOKED LIKE FOR REAL, TOO!). THE REFEREE LOOKS GENUINELY CONCERNED!

ADONIS THEN PRETENDS TO SNORT LINES OF COKE FROM OFF THE TOP ROPE!

GRABS THE MIKE AND SHOUTS:

I THINK YOU ALL SUCK!

THROWS A CHAIR INTO THE RING AT THE ANNOUNCER!

WHAT THE HELL ARE YOU DOING?!

4

The Reticent Heart

THE SECURITY GUARDS ESCORT HIM OUT BUT NOT BEFORE HE PICKS A FIGHT WITH A GUY IN THE AUDIENCE, THEN WITH A SECURITY GUY! THE LAST WE SAW OF ADONIS CHIEF JAY STRONGBOW WAS DRAGGING HIM OUT...

AFTER THINGS HAVE FINALLY SETTLED DOWN A BIT, THE RING ANNOUNCER ANNOUNCES THE MATCHES COMING UP NEXT TIME, AND YUP, YOU GUESSED IT:

...ALSO ON THE CARD, ADRIAN ADONIS!

HE WAS A HIT!

ADONIS HAS SINCE THEN MODIFIED HIS ACT IN THAT HE'S APING THE LATE GORGEOUS GEORGE'S ROUTINE, GEORGE POSSIBLY BEING THE MOST FAMOUS GRAPPLER OF ALL TIME. THE "NEW" ADONIS IS GETTING POPULAR WITH THE FANS NOW. SIGH, I GUESS YOU JUST NEVER KNOW, HUH?

END

EPILOGUE: A TRUER STORY

HAVING BEEN SACKED BY THE WWF TWICE, ADONIS THEN BEGAN GRAPPLING IN LAS VEGAS, WHERE HE SPORTED AN EVEN SEXIER LOOK.

SO I'M BEAUTIFUL-- SO WHAT?

THERE HE SET UP HIS PRESIDENTIAL CAMPAIGN HEADQUARTERS AND WON MOST OF THE PRIMARIES ON THE WEST COAST. HIS CHANCES LOOKED GOOD.

--GORBACHEV, ME AND YOU, TWO OUT OF THREE FALLS IN A STEEL CAGE--

ADR 88

MIKE DUKAKIS CHALLENGED ADONIS TO A DEBATE, BUT ADONIS SIMPLY DRAGGED DUKAKIS INTO THE RING AND AFTER A COUPLE OF BULL-DOGS AND A BEAUTIFUL BELLY TO BELLY SUPLEX FROM OFF THE TOP TURN-BUCKLE--WELL...! JACKSON, I HEAR, WAS CLEARLY STOKED...

ADONIS BOWED OUT OF THE RACE AS THE ENTIRE CAMPAIGN WAS SIMPLY A PUBLICITY STUNT JUST TO GET HIM INTO THE VEGAS LOUNGES. ADONIS NOW FILLS THE VOID ELVIS HAD LEFT EMPTY FOR SO LONG...

LOVE ME TENDER..

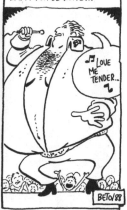

BETO/88

Gilbert Hernandez

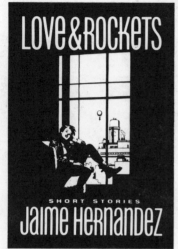